THE

INHERITANCE

& OTHER EERIE

TALES

JOHN DYBLE

This is dedicated to my lovely partner Kim who has been a constant source of encouragement.

CONTENTS

THE INHERITANCE

It was a day Henry Coombs was not looking forward to. A meeting with the solicitor to unveil the details of his late father's will was not an event he would relish, only because he knew he had the foresight to anticipate what the solicitor was likely to tell him. Coombs and his father had not been on speaking terms for some years following accusations of stealing which Coombs had strongly denied. So he was not expecting much if anything. Even at his hospital bedside in his dying moments, there had been no hint of reconciliation despite the best efforts of Coombs and his wife Laura. Although that in itself had been a futile exercise as his father's dementia was so far advanced that communication was nigh on impossible. His skeletal frame ravaged by disease was an image that would always be difficult to banish from his memory.

Feelings of remorse crept over him like a spider ensnaring its prey as the secretary ushered Laura and himself into the solicitor's room. Raising his balding head from analysing the will, Mr Brunswick introduced himself and welcomed his clients to the meeting, offering his condolences for his late client's passing. After pausing for a few moments to collect his thoughts, Brunswick began to summarise the contents of the will.

"As you probably know, your father was a staunch supporter of animal welfare. So much so that he has left most of his estate to various animal trusts. He has however set aside a few thousand pounds each for your children, Stacy and Robin Coombs, which will remain in trust until they reach the age of 21 in a few years." Henry Coombs was not surprised at what he was hearing. Brunswick fell silent for a moment before continuing. "You may or may not be aware that he owned a dwelling in the village of Riverton in Sussex for a number of years – Coombs Cottage, inherited from his father. He has left that property to you. Here are two keys and a map to locate it."

Coombs couldn't believe what he was hearing.

"I never knew he had a property in Sussex, he never mentioned it," he exclaimed.

"Well, it's here in black and white," commented Brunswick, reassuring his client that it did exist.

To say Coombs was surprised was an understatement; he was even a touch excited at his unexpected acquisition. Maybe Coombs senior wasn't as vindictive as Coombs had previously thought, despite the breakdown in their relationship all those years ago.

"I bet that surprised you Henry," said Laura as they made their way out of the solicitors.

"Definitely," replied Henry. "I'm still curious as to why he never mentioned it when he was alive," he added.

"Perhaps the cottage is haunted!" retorted Laura in a jocular manner.

"You could well be right love," responded Coombs amidst peals of laughter. "I wouldn't put it past the old devil to curse us from beyond the grave."

"I suppose you will be keen to visit the property as soon as possible," said Laura as they climbed into their car to go home.

"Yes, I am somewhat excited at the prospect. I think I'll go this coming weekend whilst you're visiting your parents."

At home in his study, Coombs carefully examined the map and keys the solicitor had given him. The map's yellow appearance and fragility suggested it was printed a good few years ago. Closer inspection, aided by a magnifying glass, revealed that its year of birth was 1939! Fortunately, the detail was still intact, but Coombs opened the map carefully to avoid possible disintegration. Given its age, Coombs was puzzled as to why the solicitor had given him such an old map when a recent one would be more relevant. Fortunately, Coombs had a new edition. Laying them side by side, a comparison of the two revealed that whilst the later map naturally showed newer roads, the older one included some that were no longer in existence. Riverton itself was evident only on the old map and not on the newer one. "How strange is that," murmured Coombs. But on further examination it became clear that it was more a hamlet than a village and presumably its few inhabitants had simply moved away or passed on. After further scrutiny, Coombs identified the likely position, some 10 miles north of Hastings.

*

Coombs had planned meticulously for his journey, which would take him some miles away from his home in Essex. As well as carrying a few provisions, he had booked two nights at the Black Wolf hostelry near to the likely location of the cottage. He considered this a wise precaution as he had no idea of the property's state of habitation. So, on a damp, dull November Saturday, Coombs weaved his way south in his ancient Ford Cortina. The intensity of the increasing rainfall threatened to penetrate the windscreen and the wipers struggled in vain to cope with the monsoon-like conditions as Coombs guided his car gingerly onto the A21. Poor visibility reduced the car's speed to a mere crawl at times much to Coombs' consternation – he was not the most patient of individuals. Within a short while, however, the rain cleared away and was replaced by glorious late afternoon sunshine that illuminated the glistening wet tarmac as the Cortina picked up speed.

Eventually, Coombs spotted a B-road turn-off for Pemberton where the Black Wolf was located. The sun was beginning to set as he pulled into the weed-ridden shingle carpark at the rear of the pub. The building's outward appearance suggested that little effort had been made to preserve its condition. Still, he was only there a couple of nights and as long as it met his needs that was all that mattered.

A blast of warm air brushed his face as he stepped across the threshold and into an atmosphere of active conversations among the residents within. "Good evening sir, how can I help you?" said the beaming barman, obviously keen to make a good impression. Formalities exchanged, Coombs was shown to his room which was clean and comfortable; once he had refreshed himself, he slipped down to the bar for a pre-dinner drink.

*

Sitting close to a few of the elderly patrons, Coombs saw the perfect opportunity to gain some local knowledge to help his quest to locate the cottage, which may prove more fruitful than following his own line of pursuit. A lull in the conversation provided the perfect moment.

"Do any of you gentlemen know where I can find Riverton, please? I'm trying to trace a cottage left to me by my late father."

They glanced at each other with a solemn look. "No longer exists my friend, except for a few empty buildings. A badly damaged German bomber ploughed through the village destroying most of the dwellings after an altercation with a Spitfire during the war. All the crew died when the plane subsequently burst into flames," said the nearest person, whose aged appearance suggested he may have been around during that time.

"Complete carnage it was," another chipped in. "Quite a few villagers were also killed and those that remained left in later years."

"How tragic," said Coombs in a sympathetic manner.

"Many generations had grown up in that village," said another.

Curiosity aroused, Coombs asked why the remaining inhabitants had left. There was a long pause in the conversation before the original speaker answered. "In later years, rumour has it that ghosts of the bomber crew were often seen in the houses that remained intact. Scared the living daylights out of the inhabitants so they fled the village never to return."

Coombs produced the original map pinpointing the likely position of Coombs Cottage and showed it to the local residents.

"It may be one of those buildings on the outskirts, if it still exists," said one. "To find the village, you need to turn right out of the pub and about a mile or so down the road you'll see the decayed remains of a lane on the left with an old signpost pointing towards what's left of the village."

"Hopefully you'll find what you are looking for," added another.

Coombs thanked those present and finished his drink before moving to the dining area to consume his evening meal. And all the time, he couldn't help thinking that the late William Coombs was teasing him from beyond the grave, and that all he would find was likely to be a crumbled ruin. Coombs found it difficult to suppress a chuckle, much to the slight amusement of his fellow diners.

*

Invigorated by a hearty breakfast the following morning, Coombs set off on the suggested route. Within a mile or so, he spotted a worn signpost with faded lettering pointing the way down a crumbling mix of fauna and concrete. It was obvious that little traffic had passed down the lane for a considerable time as weeds constantly punctuated the broken tarmac that twisted down into the barren undulating countryside through thickets of overgrown hedges and misshapen trees. Their twisted branches presented a grotesque image that threatened to engulf his vehicle as he guided his car gingerly down the lane trying to avoid obstructions that could puncture his tyres. As the vegetation began to thin out, Coombs could see outlines of crumbled structures appearing in the distant. "Riverton," he murmured.

Drawing closer, the lane widened and remains of damaged houses came into view on either side, a number of which had succumbed to infestations of weeds and decay. It was a grim sight. Coombs brought his car to a halt near what appeared to be a crossroads at the bottom of the lane curving to the left and right off the main street and giving the village the layout of an anchor if viewed from above. Only when he stepped out onto the worn tarmac could he fully absorb the desolation that surrounded him. Despite the passage of time, the devastation affected by the German aircraft was still evident as Coombs strode down the decayed road. All that remained of a number of dwellings were decimated lower and dividing walls, the bomber having completely ripped away the upper rooms and roofs on its descent that fateful night. Coombs shuddered to think of the horrific scenes the villagers had endured.

Having failed to locate his cottage on the main road, he retraced his steps and took the left turn at the crossroads. Here a number of dwellings appeared to be intact, mercifully spared by the bomber's downward flight. Covered in overgrown brambles and other creeping vegetation, the old cottages looked like they were enveloped in camouflage. The outlines of the buildings were barely recognisable.

Just as Coombs was beginning to feel his journey was wasted, he spotted a rotten signpost overgrown with ivy and with the words "Coombs Cottage" vaguely visible in faded lettering. It was just past the last building and pointed down another lane; more like a wide rough track, it snaked through a small wood. Encouraged by this discovery, Coombs quickened his pace and, within a few hundred yards, a large oval weed-infested shingle clearing appeared in front of a thatched two-storey cottage with tiny square windows and an imposing oak entrance door. The last habitation must have been some while ago as triffid-like growth had spread up the faded white walls and large cobwebs as big as small fishing nets were draped over the windows. Surprisingly, the exterior structure appeared to be sound with little evidence of decay. The house was totally unlike any of the other properties within the vicinity.

A twist of the right key and the imposing door eventually yielded though it took excessive physical force, much to Coombs' annoyance. It was as though a presence within was resisting his entry. A musty smell greeted Coombs as he stepped into a gloomy interior created by the minuscule windows which restricted any natural light. His groping hand located a light switch in the gloom, but no illumination came forth, indicating that the power supply was off. Fortunately, Coombs had brought a torch with him so further investigation could continue.

To the left and right of the hallway in which Coombs stood were a large kitchen and an adjacent bathroom and a similarly commodious living room. At the end of the hall was a stairway leading to the upper rooms. Climbing the creaking stairs brought Coombs to three rooms on the upper floor. Two bedrooms and a third room. Access to that room was denied by a locked door, which the other key did not fit. "Hmm," thought Coombs, "I wonder why."

Despite the building's age, the decor throughout the ground floor rooms smacked of the 1950s. Surprisingly, the interior was reasonably clean, except for the floor, thanks to dust sheets that were prominent in every room ensuring all the furniture was adequately protected. This pleased Coombs. He began searching for documents and any other keys, especially one for the third room upstairs. A logical place to start was the bureau in the living room. Nothing. The kitchen table drawer, however, proved more productive. But not in the way you would expect. There was nothing in the drawer – it was only when it proved troublesome to push back in that he discovered the reason. A largish brown envelope has been stuck to the underside of the table and had been worked loose by the drawer. It was as though the envelope was purposefully hidden away. "Why?" thought Coombs.

Within the envelope were several old, faded photos of what appeared to be family members.

Coombs vaguely recognised his grandfather and his grandmother. But he had always thought his father was an only child. Yet the photos clearly showed another child, a pretty young girl in her teens with long black hair. On the reverse of the photos "Summer 1925" was scrawled in black, faded ink. "Who is the mystery girl and what happened to her?" thought Coombs. Curiosity aroused, he scoured the dwelling looking for the elusive key. Nothing. Perhaps it was hidden somewhere in the bureau. Removing and examining all the drawers and looking inside of the structure however proved fruitless.

Exasperated by his failure to locate it, Coombs extended his exploration to the outside. The other key opened the kitchen door which led out to a sizeable garden bordered by large shrubs on either side of an overgrown lawn where the grass was fighting a losing battle against rampant weeds. Slicing through this green space was a winding shingle footpath that sloped down to a rusty gate. To the left of the path just before the gate was a raised mound of earth smothered in weeds with a crude wooden cross with the words "Lavinia Coombs 1912–1936" roughly etched into the wood. The garden footpath opened up onto another rough track that snaked itself through a small wood. With no desire to go any farther, Coombs retraced his steps and headed back. As he walked up the path, he noticed a trapdoor leading to a cellar; almost camouflaged amongst a large infestation of weeds, it was close to the back door of the cottage. No wonder he didn't spot it on his outward journey.

The gathering gloom reminded Coombs that the hour was getting late so he decided to suspend his exploits for the day and continue in the morning. As he moved to exit the cottage, he swore he heard distant movement from within but was unable to pinpoint exactly where. Maybe he was hearing things. An eerie silence seemed to engulf the vicinity as he made his way back to his car through the decimated village. An uneasiness crept over his being and he quickened his pace. It was as though an invisible presence was close by. Once he was within the comforting space of his vehicle, he felt a sense of relief as he fired the engine up and headed back to the Black Wolf.

*

The early morning chatter of birds woke him from his slumbers the next day. Once he had consumed his breakfast he headed back to the cottage, but not before ringing his wife Laura to update her on his progress.

First port of call was the cellar. Coombs was eager

to see what was within. Once he had removed the layers of stubborn weeds, he discovered a wooden cross securing the two trapdoors. Once this was removed, and not without some effort, he flung the doors open to be met by a rush of stale stagnant air that nearly bowled him over with its sheer obnoxiousness. Crude worn wooden steps led down into the forbidding dark interior. A short descent brought him to the cellar floor. With only the shafts of natural light restricted by the cellar opening to illuminate his way, Coombs switched on his torch to survey the surroundings. Old, dilapidated furniture strewn everywhere met his gaze as he surveyed his gloomy surroundings. In the middle of the room was a wooden ladder that reached up into the room above. Alas, entry was thwarted by another trapdoor, seemingly locked on the other side. Sweeping his torch beam around revealed what appeared to be numerous small white animal bones scattered across the wooden floor. "How in heaven's name did they get in here?" thought Coombs.

One corner of the room housed a pile of old suitcases that were probably in vogue at the start of the last century, but that were now smothered by a thick layer of dust. They sat on a large piece of stained wool carpet which Coombs stumbled over in the dim light. The movement of the carpet revealed some loose floorboards which had clearly been inserted to hide something. Removing them revealed a small hollow containing a well-worn grime-coated brown briefcase of a more recent vintage, which Coombs took into his possession for later examination. As he started to ascend the cellar steps, he could have sworn he heard a kind of shuffling sound, as though something was being dragged across the floor behind him. A quick flash of the torch beam revealed nothing. Dismissing it as a figment of his imagination, he emerged from the cellar's claustrophobic surroundings and headed into the cottage.

*

Back in the kitchen, Coombs examined the case in more detail. Entry was initially denied by the presence of a rusty lock, but a few vigorous thrusts of an old kitchen knife proved successful. A wide smile spread across Coombs' face as he observed that further keys lay within, next to what appeared to be a notebook, although its condition had deteriorated somewhat. Why had the case been hidden away? Perhaps the reason would be found within the yellow faded pages of the aforementioned book.

Coombs' interest, however, quickly transferred

back to the keys. One of which, he was thrilled to discover, opened the door to the third bedroom. Though that was not accomplished without some effort because the door was unusually heavy. Once inside, he was again met with a waft of stale air, so oppressive that he moved to open the window to let some fresh air in. This task was only accomplished following the removal of some wooden slats that had been nailed across it. "How odd," thought Coombs as he accidentally broke a small piece of glass in the corner of the frame in the course of said task. Pulling aside a worn rug on the bedroom floor revealed the locked trapdoor that led down into the cellar below. Fortunately, one of the other keys opened the padlock, enabling Coombs to pull back the door to show the descending ladder. "How long has the cottage been uninhabited?" pondered Coombs.

The bedroom was quite small compared to the other upper rooms. A tiny bed in one corner, a small wardrobe and chair in another plus an array of toys scattered everywhere suggested it was a child's room. Unlike in the other rooms, no dust sheets covered this furniture, hence the proliferation of dust. What did catch his eye in no uncertain terms was the large gold-edged portrait that dominated the wall directly opposite the entrance. The image was of a young woman dressed in a black dress reminiscent of fashion of an earlier time. She had flowing black lustrous hair, china doll features and huge blue eyes of the most unusual luminosity that Coombs had ever seen. She was breathtakingly beautiful. In her arms she protectively cradled an infant whose features were quite indistinct. It was as though they had been deliberately scrubbed out. In one corner of the picture the letters LC were discreetly scrawled so as not to detract from the beauty of the image. This appeared to be the same woman in the old photo found in the kitchen drawer and was presumably the woman buried in the back garden.

The shadows began to lengthen as the day drew towards a conclusion. A chill wind began to whistle in and around the cottage as Coombs returned to the kitchen. The lack of heating and light were beginning to make their presence felt so Coombs opted to take the briefcase back to the warmer surroundings of the Black Wolf but not before securing the doors and open window.

Following a very welcome evening meal, Coombs retired to his room, impatient to read the notebook. His south-facing room had glorious views of the undulating countryside with swathes of farmland punctuated by rows of hedges that flowed over the land like large green snakes. Dominating the rising farmland was a large oak tree with long twisting branches that appeared to reach up to the heavens. At its base was a rustic wooden bench. And on it, seemingly gazing in Coombs' direction, appeared to be a lady, although the distance hampered an accurate identification. After briefly turning away to extract the notebook from the briefcase, he happened to glance again outside but the lady had gone from the bench and was nowhere in the vicinity. "How odd," Coombs thought. "How could she disappear so quickly?" He put her out of his mind and immersed himself in the book. The diction was not easy to follow. It suggested that the uneven writing had been quickly committed to paper as though the writer was running out of time. And it made for rather uncomfortable reading.

*

"If you are reading these notes you have found the keys which I had desperately tried to conceal in the vain hope that the being that once lurked within this dwelling would never be discovered. God willing, the passage of years should have starved the thing to death so it can longer spread misery and death to those close to it. Why oh why did I allow my lovely Lavinia to travel halfway across the world to be with a man of unknown origin whose unholy union gave birth to the creature that grew into the obscenity that was a blight on humankind? I curse the fateful day she met him. I thought there was something not quite right about him. Admittedly he was ridiculously tall and well built, bronzed, young and handsome. However, the unusual wide mouth and pointed teeth and peculiar piercing oval shaped blue eyes suggested a sinister countenance that was hard to fathom. It was as though he was not of this earth. But Abram oozed charm by the bucketful and Lavinia was captivated. A whirlwind courtship ensued and within a few weeks they were married. Subsequently they took up temporary residence in the cottage with Celia and I whilst they searched for a home of their own. Shortly after, however, he had to return to his home in the Far East to be with his father who was terminally ill, or so we were told, but Abram never returned to witness the birth of his child despite countless letters that Lavinia sent which remained unanswered.

"Lavinia endured a prolonged and difficult birth but ultimately she was blessed with a baby girl who appeared to be unnaturally larger than your average baby which no doubt was responsible for the troublesome delivery. Initially there was nothing to suggest that the girl was affected in any way but, as the weeks passed, she, Liza, began to grow and grow rapidly. And as her features developed, the abnormalities were beginning to show. The arms and legs were longer than you would expect, and muscular like a man. The strange oval eyes and wide expansive mouth were clearly inherited from her father. But Lavinia didn't seem to notice. She was completely captivated by her first born despite the child's unusual development. By the time of her first birthday, Liza was as big as a small teenager, largely due to her unnatural prodigious appetite for food, mainly meat, but her speech was still that of a young child. The craving continued unabated until things reached a head as Liza approached her second birthday. Now the size of a small adult, Liza ventured into the back garden to seemingly play with our dog when for no reason she closed her large hands around its neck and strangled it. Worse was to follow as she began devouring lumps of flesh ripped from the corpse as though she hadn't eaten for months. Celia and I couldn't believe our eyes. But without hesitation we dragged Liza away from the dog and promptly locked her in her bedroom. Such was her strength it took the both of us to overpower her and confine her to her room. Thank God Lavinia was not around to witness that terrible event.

"On returning from visiting friends, Lavinia was made aware of the awful incident that had occurred a few hours earlier. Shocked beyond belief, she ventured upstairs to see her first born, finding it hard to believe what she had done. Our warning to be careful appeared to fall on deaf ears as she tentatively opened the door. 'Mama, Mama, I've missed you so much,' shouted Liza as she embraced her mother with her long muscular arms. But that initial warm greeting soon gave way to a look of malice and evil intent. 'You must never leave me Mama,' Liza scowled. 'Stop it Liza, you're suffocating me,' wailed Lavinia as Liza continued to use her unnatural strength to squeeze the life out of her mother. Sensing Lavinia was in peril, Celia and I tore up the stairs, burst into the room and, without hesitation and using superhuman effort, pulled Liza away from our fast-expiring daughter whose deathly pallor suggested we were too late. I brought Lavinia's limp frame downstairs and laid her gently on the settee whilst Celia swiftly locked the bedroom door behind us; the sound of Liza banging on the door echoed in our ears. Despite my best efforts to resuscitate her, Lavinia never drew breath again. The grief consuming Celia and I at that moment was immeasurable as we tried to console each other. We buried Lavinia close to the small wood at the bottom of our garden. She was not known in the village, hence her disappearance did not provoke any reaction from the locals.

"We should have reported the incident to the police but Liza would have ended up in an asylum and would have posed an unwelcome threat to those within. To let her run amok in society would be unforgivable. What were we to do with her? We vowed never to let her out of her room. I nailed stout wooden slats across the window and locked the trapdoor down into the cellar to prevent her exit. It was not a decision that Celia and I took lightly. After all, she was our flesh and blood. But something had to be done. After much deliberation, and God forgive us, we took it upon ourselves to let her starve. At the beginning, it was hard especially for Celia to hear her granddaughter banging on the door begging for food, but our resolve was strong and we resisted the overwhelming urge to let her out. Within a few weeks the sound of movement within the room lessened until there was silence. Had Liza drawn her last breath? Tentatively opening the door, we stepped into her room. Everything within the room was in complete disarray as though a mini whirlwind had entered the room and flung its contents everywhere. But there was no sign of Liza. Where had she gone? It was as though she had never existed. Could it be that lack of food would have the opposite effect of shrinking growth as opposed to increasing it, to such an extent that her size was reduced to that of a foetus or even smaller? It sounds ridiculous but if Liza's growth was unusually rapid, given her age, could not the reverse happen? It was totally irrational but what other explanation could there be? There was no sign of any forced exit from the room. And the bedroom door and the trapdoor into the cellar were both locked.

Because of the awful events that had occurred, Celia and I came to the conclusion that we could no longer reside in the cottage and we subsequently decided to return to our other residence in London.

Samuel Coombs, September 1936."

*

Coombs was totally transfixed by the nightmarish transcript he'd just read. Was it for real or the product of an overactive imagination? Either way, sleep was difficult to come by that night as he sought unsuccessfully to erase his grandfather's words from his mind. Eventually he succumbed to tiredness but not before dreaming of a lady in black standing at the foot of his bed smiling at him through pointed teeth which made him sit bolt upright in his bed in a cold sweat.

"So what did you find at the cottage Henry?" enquired Laura, keen to know what he had discovered.

"Additional keys and my grandfather's diary – it makes for grim reading," Coombs replied, eager to avail Laura of his experience at the cottage.

Once Coombs had finished telling her about his trip, Laura found it hard to believe what her husband had just told her. "Sounds like something out of a fantasy novel," she exclaimed.

"Read it for yourself," Coombs responded, agitated that perhaps she didn't believe him.

"I see what you mean Henry," said Laura, slowly coming to terms with the likelihood that the diary contents were not a figment of the writer's imagination. "To be honest Henry, I think we should just tidy the house up and sell it," she added.

"Yes that seems to be the best course of action as neither you nor I would be comfortable using it as a bolthole given its history and its remoteness," replied Coombs. "I must confess, it did give me the creeps the brief time I was there," he added.

*

Work commitments delayed a further visit to the cottage for several weeks. A room was again booked for a weekend at the Black Wolf with Coombs using a large van as his preferred mode of transport; its carrying capacity would be ideal for removing unwanted items from the cottage. He couldn't help but detect a sombre mood within the pub on arrival. Civility was as before but the atmosphere didn't appear quite as jovial. Once he had freshened up, he went to the bar for a pre-dinner pint and picked up a copy of the *Pemberton Gazette* that happened to be lying on the table in front of him. 'Horrific attack on sheep in Mordant's field' was the headline on the front page which drew his attention like a magnet. It made grim reading. Charles Mordant, making his usual weekly visit to feed his animals, was shocked to find that a few of his ewes had been killed and mutilated. Limbs had been torn off in what appeared to be a frenzied attack. "I can't believe that there are any wild animals that exist around here that could inflict such wounds," the puzzled and distressed owner had told the newspaper.

"Hard to believe something like that can happen round here," interjected the barman as he passed by collecting empty glasses.

"Yes, I agree, it's rather gruesome," replied Coombs.

"Another pint?" asked the barman, sensing Coombs' alarmed disposition.

"I think I will, thank you," answered Coombs, finding it difficult to conceal his growing uneasiness.

"Pet cats and small dogs started to mysteriously disappear a few weeks ago," said the barman. "It's rumoured that a tiger that escaped from Lessington Zoo a few miles away is the likely culprit but it hasn't been found yet," he added.

Coombs found it difficult to recall what he consumed for his evening meal as various thoughts of an unpleasant kind continued to race through his mind. It was logical to think that a big cat had committed the ghastly deeds, but Coombs felt that the real villain lay closer to home. Was it merely a coincidence that the pets vanished shortly after Coombs had left the cottage a few weeks back and that the perpetrator was now targeting larger prey to satisfy its unnatural appetite for meat? Who or what would be next on the menu? Coombs shuddered to think of the consequences. But all his trains of thought pointed to Liza as the likely perpetrator. If she had shrunk to minimal proportions, to those of a very small mammal such as a mouse or rat, which sounded ridiculous but was feasible, it would explain how she had escaped detection all those years ago. And the small area of the broken bedroom window may have been big enough for her to break out and create havoc… Coombs broke into a cold sweat as he realised that he may have been unwittingly responsible for unleashing an evil entity back into the outside world.

Whilst these thoughts were circulating through his mind, the pub door was suddenly flung open to reveal an exhausted elderly man standing in the doorway, drenched in perspiration with a frightened expression.

"Looks like you've seen a ghost Bert," said the barman. "What's up mate?" he added.

Recognising that the man was clearly traumatised and in need of assistance, Coombs rushed to his aid and guided him to a seat next to him. Consumption of a complimentary pint courtesy of the barman helped to relax Bert enough to be able to tell his tale.

"Was walking down Pipers Lane on my way here and I was just passing the old village on my left when I heard this high-pitched scream coming from the field where the cattle were grazing on my right. God it was an awful sound." Clearly shaken by his experience, he paused for a moment to drink. "When I turned round, I saw this creature, not sure if it was half human or half animal as it was getting dark, tearing a leg off a cow that was lying mortally wounded on its side as though it was tearing up paper and feasting on it. It must have sensed my presence because it glanced at me and moved in my direction.

Panic gripped me like a vice and my legs felt like they were filled with lead as I ran towards the pub, but when I looked back again just before I entered, the creature had gone. Never been so scared in my life."

Observing that Bert was in need of further lubrication, Coombs provided another pint of the man's favourite tipple to restore his shredded nerves and help him relax. The drink thankfully helped the conversation drift off onto much more palatable subjects before Bert decided to leave.

"I'll go with you Bert just to make sure you get home safely," offered Coombs.

"That's kind of you my friend," the man replied.

Coombs was met with looks of approval from the barman and other drinkers as he proceeded to escort Bert out of the pub to his home.

As they stepped out into the chill still air of an autumnal evening, the moon was so intense it illuminated the countryside as though it was daytime. Bert knew a shortcut which avoided Pipers Lane. "Don't feel comfortable going that way home tonight in view of what happened so we can cut through the small wood that runs round the back of the old village," said Bert.

"Have you lived here long Bert?" asked Coombs.

"Most of my life, been on my own the last 10 years or so since my Margery passed on God bless her," came the reply. "I've seen some strange things in my time but nothing like what I witnessed tonight," he added.

As the pair passed through the wood, the moon's shadows cast grotesque shapes through the twisted elongated branches that seemed to reach out to them as they passed by. Coombs observed lights twinkling in the distance as they emerged from the wood.

"Ah nearly home," muttered Bert as they turned down a rough track that emerged into a wide clearing adjacent to a small thatched cottage. "Fancy a cuppa before you return?" suggested the old man.

"Sound like a great idea Bert," came the reply.

Convivial conversation flowed as the two relaxed in front of a roaring fire inside Bert's comfortable cabin before Coombs recognised it was time to get back to the pub before closing time.

 Bidding his host a fond farewell, Coombs stepped out into the chill of the night. As he passed through the wood, his ears were assaulted by the echoes of a hideous high-pitched scream from behind him that shocked him beyond belief such was its intensity.

"Bert!" he shouted to himself. Without hesitation, he ran as fast as he could back towards the source of that awful noise – Bert's cottage. Heart pounding like a sledgehammer, his body covered in sweat, he pounded on the door but there was no reply. Sensing the worst, he frantically kicked the door in to find Bert's grotesquely twisted body lying prostrate on the ever-increasingly blood-stained floor. A look of utter terror was etched across his motionless face and his head was nearly severed from his neck. Coombs did his best to compose himself at the horrific scene before him as he then observed that Bert's right leg was missing, torn off completely at the hip by something or someone with immense strength. A trail of blood led up to the large shattered kitchen window, clearly the perpetrator's point of entry and exit. This was no zoo animal attack. Liza had returned but in what form?

Shock gave way to an overwhelming desire to exact revenge, to seek out the thing that had committed this awful deed and to terminate its existence. Coombs' emotions were running at stratospheric levels as his eyes scanned the room for a means of executing said deed. And as if his wish was granted, he ventured into the kitchen and found a shotgun and ammunition in a glass-fronted cabinet mounted on the wall. Loading the twin chambers, he snapped the gun shut and strode purposefully out into the night towards Coombs Cottage.

Adrenalin was running at full tilt as he approached his dwelling from the rear and noticed that the window of Liza's room, although closed, had now been completely smashed in. With his heart pounding like a runaway train, and no thought for his own safety, he entered the cottage and ascended the stairs, unlocked Liza's bedroom door and flung it open, gun in hand, ready to obliterate the thing before him. The moon flooded shafts of bright light into the room through the broken window, illuminating the sickening sight of the blood-splattered trail to the entity within.

But Coombs froze, totally transfixed. For standing before him was a creature that was hardly human. Its huge hairless head nearly brushed the ceiling and it had vivid blue oval eyes and an amphibiously wide mouth that was dripping with blood as it consumed chunks of flesh from a human leg with its razor-sharp pointed teeth. The unusually long muscular arms nearly reached the blood-soaked floor. Coombs felt powerless to act and dropped the shotgun on the floor as though he was hypnotised as the misshapen entity dropped the leg and loped towards him with a piercing look that was so evil he was able to provide no resistance as the shovel-sized hands closed around his neck, slowly suffocating the life out of him. But as Coombs felt his life ebbing away, he heard a faint voice pleading, "No Liza, no."

"Mama, Mama," muttered Liza as she swung round in the direction of the source of the sound, thus releasing her grip on Coombs' neck.

"Come to Mama, Liza, come here baby."

For in a corner of the room, emerging from the dark shadows, was the ghostly image of a tall elegant woman clad in black with long black hair, arms outstretched, enticing Liza towards her.

"Lavinia," gasped Coombs.

Liza moved towards her. At that point, Coombs regained his composure, grabbed the shotgun off the floor and fired both barrels without hesitation. Liza crumpled to the floor in an instant.

"Mama, Mama, I love you," muttered Liza with her dying breath.

The woman started to sob as she caressed the motionless figure before her. The mourning was short lived and she suddenly flashed Coombs a look of utter hatred and rose up to confront her daughter's executioner. The vivid blue eyes bore right through

Coombs as she advanced towards him. Quick as a flash, Coombs turned and exited the room, slamming the door shut. His heart was pounding uncontrollably as he stumbled down the steps to the ground floor, tipping over an oil lamp in the hallway in his hurry to escape and sending sheets of flames darting around the floor in every direction, latching on to everything that would burn. Within seconds, the flames were spreading throughout the wooden structure like wildfire.

Coombs burst through the back door and headed back to the Black Wolf, his mind in mental torment. Panting for breath, he fumbled for his room key and his shaking hand took several attempts to gain entry. Once inside, he gulped down one whiskey then another in quick succession as he tried to calm his nerves. Sleep was out of the question as he tried to contemplate the nightmarish events of the last few hours. As he began to succumb to exhaustion, the wind rose like an escalating orchestral movement, rattling the windows and whistling around the door. It was as though an invisible entity was trying to enter the room. Eventually, the wild wind gradually subsided to a gentle whisper and calm was restored. But as Coombs began to drift into drowsiness, a distinctive tapping on the window began to resonate around the room. As he opened the window, the tapping ceased. But as he pulled it shut, he felt some invisible thing brush past him and into the room. Fear gripped him like a boa constrictor for as he turned back into the room, a black shadow rose up from a corner of the room, increasing in size as it advanced towards Coombs' petrified body, its piercing oval blue eyes glowing in the dark…

*

Later the following morning, the barman observed that Coombs had failed to attend breakfast as he had done on previous days, which he thought was a little unusual. Sensing that his customer may have overslept, he went to his room. A knock on the door and a verbal question about his wellbeing failed to provoke any response. So using a duplicate key, he opened the door and entered the room. His face turned as white as a sheet and he nearly collapsed in fright at the scene before him. For on the floor lay the prostrate corpse of the late Mr Coombs. His terror-stricken bulging eyes stood out like a beacon against the grey pallor of his dead face. A post-mortem revealed that he had died of natural causes.

A HAUNTING IN HENSWORTH

J ames Holden's role as a supervisor in a shoe factory
was often a testing one. If tact, diplomacy and
assertiveness were not dispatched with equal
measure, then his tenure would be short lived.
Encouraging his team of lady employees to work
efficiently without denying them reasonable breaks
was a fine balancing act but Holden achieved it with
consummate ease. But there were times when even
his patience was stretched like an elastic band. And
this particular week had proved more stressful than
usual due to staff shortages and the need to maintain
sales targets. So it was with some relief that he
received a timely invitation to spend a few days with
his grandparents Joseph and Mary Holden in the
village of Hensworth in Yorkshire – it could not have
come at a better time. Orphaned at a young age
following his parents' tragic death in a train crash, the
young James had been brought up by the Holdens
before he struck out on his own in his late teens.

*

Piloting his Fiat Panda out of York on a late

October afternoon, James was pleased to escape his work-dominated existence following a failed relationship; a chance to catch up with his ageing relations provided welcome relief. Weaving his way through the undulating scenic countryside beneath bright blue skies provided a relaxing experience which seemed to bode well for his break. Within next to no time, he'd slipped off the motorway and was heading towards Hensworth some 20 miles away, deep in the Yorkshire Dales. The setting sun matched the Panda stride for stride as it rolled along the horizon before the car slipped down the twisting B-road into a shallow valley.

Just as dusk was approaching, a blanket of fog slowly spread across the road as James approached the stone bridge that crossed the river just before the village. As he reduced his speed to a mere crawl, a man in dishevelled attire suddenly appeared and stood motionless in the middle of the stone structure, gazing in his direction with the mist swirling around him. Braking hard, James stopped abruptly to avoid the inevitable collision. But as he stepped out of his car, the vision disappeared as quickly as it had materialised. "How odd," thought James. Satisfied it was now safe to progress, he passed over the bridge without any further incident and made his way along the winding road that bisected Hensworth with dwellings huddled together on either side as though they were keeping each other warm. After a few hundred yards, he spotted the turning to his left, next to the village post office, that brought him onto a tree-lined lane where a number of imposing 19th-century houses resided, one of which belonged to the Holden family. He turned into a wide gravel drive in front of a large Victorian two-storey house, the brickwork barely visible through the blanket of ivy that almost engulfed the entire building save the entrance door and windows.

A hefty bang of the lion-headed door knocker brought a swift response from within.

"Good evening, James, good to see you," came the bright and cheery response from Joseph Holden as he opened the door to greet his grandson.

"Good to be here grandad," replied James, wincing from Joe's firm handshake. Despite his advanced years, Holden senior cut an impressive figure. Tall, fit and seemingly alert, his apparent youthfulness betrayed his age.

"Cup of tea young man?" suggested Joe as he ushered James into the living room, offering him a seat in an expansive leather armchair, close to a large roaring fire set in an elaborate hearth. "Mary, James has arrived," shouted Joe to his spouse who was otherwise engaged upstairs.

"Ok dear," came the clear response. "I'll be down soon," she added.

James had fond memories of staying with his grandparents when he was younger – playing in their vast back garden and rambling through the large wood that edged the Holden property. They had always made James feel at home, and still did when he needed a break from the pressures of work.

"So what happened with Emily? She seemed a lovely girl," asked Joe, as forthright and direct as ever.

"We just grew apart," came the less than honest reply from James as the three of them sat close to the fire, the glowing embers reflecting off their faces. Sensing that young Holden was less than keen to discuss his personal life, Joe wisely did not pursue it.

"How was your journey down James?" asked Mary, aware that a swift change of subject was needed.

"Everything went smoothly until I approached the bridge," replied James, "and then this man in strange clothes suddenly appeared on the bridge in an agitated state amidst this swirling mist. But then he promptly disappeared when I got out of the car to check he was ok."

"Well I think we all sometimes see things which aren't really there," said Joe who was quick to dismiss the sighting as a product of James's imagination.

"Perhaps you are right grandad, the vision did come and go in just seconds," James replied, not wholly convinced. The nature of a glance between the elderly couple seemed to suggest they knew more than they were prepared to say, but James let the matter go.

"I think dinner is just about ready," said Mary, eager to change the topic again.

Appetites satisfied after a hearty dinner, the threesome spent the remainder of the evening catching up on various events each of them had experienced since they last met a few years ago. As the evening drew to a close, Mary showed James to his room. "We've given you the large bedroom that overlooks the garden and the wood beyond," Mary said. "I think you will approve of the views," she added.

With the passage of the years, James had forgotten just how vast the back garden was. Under the bright light of the full moon he could clearly see the large swathes of neatly cut dark green grass punctuated by round and oval plant beds featuring brightly coloured shrubs that seemed to come alive under the luminous gaze of the moon. A distinctive gravel path snaked its way through, finally terminating at an arched-roofed summer house located at the very top of the garden. It was a wonderful view, even more so on a bright summers day he thought. James was close to exhaustion and climbed quickly into bed. Within minutes, he fell into a deep and troubled sleep and began to dream:

There was movement within the wood that lay beyond the garden. Despite the distance, it seemed that a woman in a long hooded black coat was being closely pursued by a taller woman in similar garb with an unusual gait. A sudden gust of wind blew the hood off the pursuer to reveal a white grinning skull devoid of flesh, eyeless sockets and long tresses of jet-black hair. It made James's skin crawl. Much as he wanted to avert his gaze, he couldn't. It was as though he was totally transfixed by the scenario opening up before him. Within a few strides, the hideous entity was upon the woman just as she tried to enter the cottage, slashing at her with a sword. Within seconds, the woman collapsed to the ground, her inert body riddled with gaping wounds. The perpetrator loped off in the direction she had come from and disappeared back into the wood.

*

James woke suddenly from his nightmare and sat bolt upright, his body covered in sweat and his heart pounding like a sledgehammer. With the dream still active in his mind, he threw open the curtains, expecting to see a tragic scene. But the tranquil view was as before. Taking deep breaths, he slowly regained his composure, his heartbeat returning its pace to a calmer level. Eventually, he drifted off to sleep again only to be awoken by the chatter of birds signifying the arrival of dawn. After a quick shower, a sleep-deprived James shuffled downstairs to consume some breakfast.

"Restless night James?" asked Mary, noticing her grandson's rather tired disposition.

"You could say that Mary," sighed James. "Had quite an awful dream that seemed too close to reality for my liking. It was quite scary."

Once James had related his nightmare to his grandmother, the look on her face suggested she could throw some light on the subject.

"Well the village is notorious for events that occurred in the past – some locals have dismissed them as old wives' tales but they may relate to your dream," said Mary.

"So what happened?" asked James in an interested

and excited tone.

"You may or may not know that your grandfather and I have lived here for well over 50 years. When we were first here, it was just scrubland up to the boundary where the wood is with a small derelict cottage on the perimeter. After we built our house, we landscaped the back garden, demolished the cottage and built the summer house in the same position because it faced west and it's a lovely place to watch the setting sun. Well, when we dismantled the cottage, we found the skeleton of a woman under the old floorboards. Her clothing had been torn in numerous places, various bones were broken and there was a large hole in the top of her skull. It was quite a shock. We were so intrigued that your grandfather and I visited the local library in Mazenby, a town just a few miles away, to learn more. Thumbing through the earliest editions of the *Mazenby Gazette* revealed that a certain Marion Moncur was accused of practising the black arts in Hensworth in 1860 and condemned to death by burning at the stake. The story goes that she was betrayed by her lover William Blake after she terminated their relationship on the eve of their engagement. Before the flames began to consume her body, she shrieked out a curse that Blake, his family and any of his line would meet a terrible end. Those in attendance said that the look of pure evil on Moncur's face made their blood run cold as she continued her vengeful tirade until the escalating flames finally silenced her. Her ashes were sealed in a wooden box and buried down an old disused well in the wood which was filled with stones to supposedly prevent the resurrection of her evil spirit. Or so the story goes."

"Wow, that is scary!" exclaimed James, absolutely captivated by the unfolding tale.

After pausing for a moment, Mary then continued. "A few years later, William married Sarah, the daughter of the local baker, and they built a cottage just where the summer house is. But as time went by, less and less was seen of Sarah, and William's deteriorating mental state and insularity was a growing concern. Things came to a head one night when a fear-stricken William supposedly rushed out of his cottage as though he was being pursued, ran down the main street, constantly looking behind him, lost his footing and fell off the bridge and drowned in the fast-flowing river. His body was never found. Despite a thorough search of the cottage, there was no trace of Sarah either. It was as though she had simply vanished. The villagers shunned the cottage thereafter, convinced that it was haunted and it remained empty until we demolished it."

Eagerly interrupting, James asked: "So were the remains under the floorboards Sarah's?"

"Sadly they were, a tarnished ring was found on her left hand with the initials SB engraved on it," replied Mary.

"So who killed her?" enquired James.

"Circumstantial evidence suggests that Blake murdered her in one of his violent rages brought on by his mental condition and buried her under the cottage. The tool of execution was never found, but the nature of his subsequent demise points to him as the likely suspect, although it has never been proven that he committed the deed," answered Mary. "Joseph doesn't like talking about the village's spooky past, hence his reluctance to engage with you last night about the incident on the bridge," she added.

"That was some tale Mary," said James, his fascination with Hensworth's past evident to see.

Eager to explore the surrounding countryside, James finished his breakfast, bid farewell to his grandmother and stepped out into the chilly autumn air, well insulated from the elements. His planned route would take him through the picturesque back garden and into the wood with a stop at The Stag hostelry in the village for light refreshment before returning to his grandparents' house. The sun ascended slowly through the puffs of light cloud as his feet crunched along the loose shingle of the path winding through the back garden. James couldn't help but admire the work that Joe and Mary had done in designing a really beautiful area awash with vibrant coloured shrubs and flowers. As he circumvented the last shrub border at the top of the garden, the summer house came into view. It was bathed in bright sunlight and James couldn't resist opening the French doors and relaxing for a moment on one of the comfy chairs that faced the garden. Protected from the excesses of autumnal weather, the house provided some unexpected late morning warmth. As he admired the view across the garden, he heard footsteps approaching. Expecting to see his grandmother appear, he stepped outside to greet her. But there was no one there and the footsteps stopped. "How strange," he thought. Without giving the incident any further thought, he resumed his journey through an opening in the laurel hedge that bordered the garden and headed into the wood that lay beyond.

As James strode along the little-used rough grass footpath that snaked through the undergrowth, the density of trees seemed to thicken, allowing only thin shafts of sunlight to penetrate the increasing gloom. In a short while, he came upon an open space, its centre dominated by a moss-encrusted circular stone well filled with stone. Brushing aside the debris revealed a flat stone slab in the centre. On it was roughly etched the following: "Here-in lies the remains of Marion Moncur, servant of Satan and evil witch of this parish, and here she must stay". For some inexplicable reason, James recited the inscription in a loud voice; his words were accompanied by the sound of a rising wind rustling through the trees, close to his very person. When he finished, the wind died away. Feeling distinctly uncomfortable, he resumed his journey at a quicker pace and felt a sense of relief as he emerged from the wood and headed up a meandering lane that climbed a hill with glorious views over the open farmland. When he stopped briefly at the summit to admire the scenery, he noticed a tall dark shadow standing at the point where minutes before he had exited the wood. As he began his descent, he happened to glance back. Nothing there. "Really must pull myself together," he murmured as he ventured on to The Stag at the bottom of the hill.

*

The public house was bustling with activity as James pushed his way through the dense mass of bodies en route to the bar. Pint and pie in hand he jostled towards what seemed to be the only vacant seat.

"Never seen this place so busy," exclaimed the elderly man sitting next to him.

"You come here regularly then?" replied James, keen to strike up a conversation.

"Yes, this is my daily haunt," he replied. "When you've been around as long as I have young man, you welcome a bit of company in your later years."

"Have you lived in the village for a long time?" enquired James.

"Most of my life, never been that far away"

"I'm just spending a few days with my grandparents, Mary and Joseph Holden who live nearby."

The old man's eyes lit up. "Ah, the Holdens, the couple who found a woman's skeleton under old Blake's cottage on their land many years ago, if my memory serves me well. Was front page news back then."

"My grandparents thought her husband William Blake killed her," said James, hoping that the old man might add something to James's knowledge of the incident.

"The story handed down through my previous generations is that Blake spent much of his time fishing at the small lake in Witches Wood, much to Sarah's consternation. Furious rows erupted between the pair and when Sarah mysteriously disappeared, rumours spread that Blake had done away with her. But it was never proven. His subsequent suicide, however, suggested that he was the perpetrator."

"How did Witches Wood get its name?" interjected James, pretending he knew little.

"It's an old wives' tale but it seems a woman was accused of consorting with the devil and was burned at the stake in the middle of the wood and her remains were buried there," replied the old man. "Rumour has it that her ghost roams the wood and heaven help anybody who happens to cross her path."

"How creepy," said James, casting his mind back to his recent experience. "I know this may sound crazy but has anybody actually seen her?" enquired James, eager to know more.

The old man paused for a moment. "A local man Harold Wesley came out of the wood late one evening in a terrible mental state claiming that something or someone was chasing him. It affected him so badly that his family had him committed to an asylum," came the reply.

"How awful!" exclaimed James, beginning to wish he had never asked.

"Well it's time for me to go home for my afternoon nap," said the old man as he rose to leave. "Nice to have met you young Holden – and avoid the wood after dark," he added as he walked out of the pub.

*

James felt a little unsettled after the man's last remark, but his previous comments seemed to provide an answer as to why Blake had acted completely out of character in the actions he took. His murderous deeds were clearly activated by the curse unleashed by Marion Moncur wreaking her revenge from beyond the grave. It made James's blood run cold just thinking of it. Conscious of the old man's remarks, James opted to take the longer route home, via the back lane, as he stepped out of the pub into the winter chill. Dusk was approaching fast as the sun was beginning to set. Striding along at pace it wasn't long before he found the entrance to his grandparents' house. Once inside, a sense of relief swept over him like a warm blanket, knowing that he had safely arrived back, but at the same cursing himself for believing in old folk lore.

"Did you have a good day, James?" asked Mary as he swept into the living room and made himself comfortable in the armchair closest to the inviting warmth of the glowing log fire.

"Yes grandma, very interesting," he replied.

"Tell me more," Mary said, as she joined James with a much-needed cup of tea for both of them.

He regaled Mary with the key points of his conversation with the old man in The Stag. Reflecting on her grandson's comments, Mary paused for a moment before responding. "It may take some believing, but the story goes that it was the spirit of Marion Moncur that possessed Blake to murder Sarah and, when he realised what he'd done, he buried her in the cottage to escape detection. Filled with remorse, he later took his own life," said Mary, noticing the avid interest on her grandson's face.

"Have there been any strange happenings since?" asked James, totally captivated.

"None that I know of," replied his grandmother, "but as you seem so interested in the village's folklore, you may want to visit the library in Mazenby to find out more," she added.

"Sounds like a good idea, I think I'll give the

library a visit tomorrow," he replied.

"Good for you James. I'm sure you'll enjoy it."

*

After dinner and another convivial evening with his grandparents, James retired early ready for his exploits the following day. Blessed with uninterrupted sleep, he felt more energised than he did the previous morning. Mary and Joe were off to York to do some shopping so provided James with a key to get in if he returned before them. The rain was lashing down with a vengeance as James guided his car gingerly along the narrow rain-soaked tarmac towards Mazenby, a small town a few miles away. Hindered by the inclement weather, the journey seemed to take an eternity but eventually he was ensconced within the library, marvelling at the wealth of history at his disposal. His eyes lit up when he unintentionally came across the lineage of the Blake family. It transpired that William Blake was the eldest by some years of three siblings, the others being Edith and George. Edith had married Arthur Holden, a local farmer, and given birth late in life to twin boys, Joseph and Charles. So William Blake was his great-great-uncle! James was stunned by this revelation. There were some grim entries. Arthur suffered a grisly end when

51

he was crushed by a tractor, Edith succumbed to a mysterious illness in her later years, George was killed by shrapnel on the western front in Belgium in 1918 and Charles, a Spitfire pilot, was killed instantly when his plane was blown apart by ground artillery over France in 1944. Such was James's fixation with the history of the Blake family, albeit a sad one, that it curtailed his further interest in Hensworth's folklore. A cold sweat slowly crept over James when he realised that Marion Moncur's curse had come true as one by one the Blake lineage had met an untimely death, including his own parents! Considering the counter-argument, however, he realised that the nature of their deaths was not particularly unusual, and it was too easy to believe that the witch's curse was responsible. Furthermore, the fact that his grandparents were still alive and kicking seemed to weaken the curse theory even more. However, James still found it difficult to believe there was no link as he drove back to his grandparents' house, his mind totally consumed by the history of the Blake dynasty.

*

As his car turned into the Holdens' driveway, the sun had slid beyond the horizon to be replaced by the black veil of darkness. His grandparents had yet to return. This didn't particularly bother James as it was likely he would return before them given his short sojourn at the library. And it gave him the opportunity to dip into the vast library of books that were present in the living room. Once he had selected a book, he was soon immersed in its content. So much so that the hours seemed to slip away. This tranquillity was rudely disturbed by a knocking on the front door. On the doorstep stood two policemen with solemn looks on their faces.

"Are you related to Mr and Mrs Holden?"

"Yes," replied James. "I'm their grandson, why what has happened?" he added in a tone that suggested he feared the worst.

"I'm afraid their car left the road at Highbury Corner, struck a tree and killed them both outright."

James couldn't believe what he was hearing, yet in strange kind of way he was not totally surprised. After recovering his composure, James asked what may have caused the accident.

"Difficult to say at this stage sir until we do a full enquiry. The road conditions were fine and there was no other car involved," replied the policeman. "We will need you to make a formal identification of the bodies in due course," he added.

"Fully understand officer," said James, still trying

to come to terms with his grandparents' fate.

*

After reassuring the officers that he was fine being left on his own despite the devastating news, he consumed a large glass of red wine to help him cope with the awful news. He knew his grandfather was a decent driver and never took any risks, so aside from a sudden health or car issue, it was difficult to fathom why their car had left the road. Far be it for James to consider that that a witch's curse would carry any weight in the modern world. Who would believe in such things? James downed a further glass of wine to help him relax. Of course, he now knew his existence may well be under threat as the sole surviving member of the Blake clan. But how could the curse be broken? Perhaps the answer was within one of the books in his grandparents' library. Thumbing through row upon row of aged tomes, his bruised fingers finally pulled out "Witches and Demons" by A G Porter, which had annoyingly been filed in the wrong place, delaying its procurement.

After the consumption of much-needed refreshments, including further wine, James retired to the most comfortable armchair in the living room which was awash with the vivid light from the glowing flames of the warm fire. Despite his relatively high intake of alcohol, his patience was never in doubt as he ploughed through page upon page due to the absence of an index, a feature which betrayed the book's ancient origins. The brittleness of the pages was a hindrance he could have done without as he delicately turned each of them with care.

The house began to creak and groan as gusts of wind escalated outside, causing the flames in the hearth to dart around like demented dancers as pockets of breeze hurtled down the chimney. Uncannily, one of these reached out into the room and blew aside a number of pages, much to James's annoyance. But when the breeze stopped, the pages were open at extracts that proved to be useful. How unreal was that? It was as though an invisible entity had been sent to aid James in his quest. Looking through the extract in detail, he found the relevant script. The faded spidery entries and complicated old English were not easy to follow, but James somehow managed to make sense of it. It seemed that to banish the witch's curse forever, the box and ashes must be taken to a place of worship where a man of god must cast the spirit out and the ashes must subsequently be scattered into the sea on the ebb tide. All these deeds must be executed within 12 hours. At least now he had a plan of action.

*

Sleep was not easy to come by that evening. The combination of alcohol and the persistent wind howling in and around the house did their best to thwart his slumber. Not surprisingly, he woke late the next morning, slightly the worse for wear but totally focused on the task ahead. Armed with a shovel, he ventured into the wood. Bathed in bright sunshine, the close-knit banks of tall trees took on a less sinister look as James made his way to the stone well. Reaching the clearing, he removed the stone plaque from the top of the stone-packed well and began to excavate. This coincided with a gentle rustling of the circle of trees facing the well that increased in intensity with each thrust of the shovel. It was as though a presence was reacting to the disturbance. Oblivious to the escalating noise, James pressed on and, within minutes, the decaying casket emerged. Discarding his shovel, he pulled the casket out and made his was way back to the house. He glanced at his watch – 11am; by this time tomorrow, the task would be complete and the curse removed. James felt rather smug. Plenty of time to complete the remaining tasks he thought.

The casket was about the size of a small shoe box;

it was nailed shut and there were curious markings on the lid. Time and the nails' susceptibility to damp provided little resistance to James's well-directed thrusts with a chisel. The opening of the box released an obnoxious but thankfully short-lived odour. The thick layer of blackened ashes seemed to have a hold over James for a brief moment before he quickly closed the lid. Wasting no time, James headed for Hensworth church where, fortunately, the vicar was in residence. Briefly explaining his predicament, James showed him the guidance for the eradication of the curse.

"Normally an exorcism would suffice, but this is a very evil spirit, hence the need to do more," sighed the vicar. Once the exorcism was executed, the vicar returned the box to James with a warning. "Make sure you beat the deadline, otherwise the spirit will continue to be active."

"Consider it done," replied a buoyant James.

Next stop was Mazenby library. As he browsed through the tide times, his face turned to a frown. The ebb tide today would peak at 3pm – the next one would be too late. He needed to release the ashes by 3pm. And it was now 1.45pm. With no time to lose, James rushed out of the library and headed for the nearest shore at Newton, an hour away, depending on the traffic. Feeling slightly anxious, he propelled his car as fast as conditions would allow with grim determination. Pulling into a carpark, James checked his watch – 2.50pm. He had made it. He ran onto the beach, down to the shoreline and into the water up to his knees before opening the casket and hurling the ashes into the receding sea with two minutes to spare. Gasping for air, he stood motionless in the water, threw the casket away, rested his hands on his waist and breathed a huge sigh of relief...

*

Tom Bradley, out for his usual mid-afternoon walk, strode purposefully along the shoreline close to the water's edge, his boots making a satisfying crunch in the moist sand as he approached Newton Spit, a stretch of shrub-encrusted sand dune that reached out into the water. As he rounded the small peninsula, a small crescent-shaped bay opened up before him. In the distance, he could see a person standing in the sea at the other end of the bay, arm raised in the act of throwing something into the sea. Conscious of the time, he happened to glance at his watch – 3.05pm. When he looked again, he observed a tall, emaciated woman with long black hair suddenly emerge from the nearby wood, brandishing a long sword and coming up swiftly behind the person in the sea. Fearing the worst, Bradley started to run as quick as he could, shouting as loud as his vocal chords would allow to warn the intended victim. Alas, it was too late. Frenzied blow upon blow reigned down upon the hapless man who collapsed into the sea within seconds. As Tom closed to within a few yards, the hooded being glanced in his direction, blood dripping off the sword's blade, and then returned at pace from whence she had come. Bradley gasped in horror. The image of a grinning skull with eyeless sockets proved too much and he promptly fainted. When he came to a while later, there was no evidence of the awful scene he had just witnessed; the man in the sea had disappeared completely. There was no blood on the sand either. Was it a figment of his imagination ? He hardly knew what he had seen. But Tom began to doubt his own sanity. He never uttered a word to anybody about what he'd seen. Who would believe him? But future walks were taken in other directions and never along that bay. Ever again.

THE GOLD WHISTLE

The sky was dark and overcast on a damp September day and you could hear a penny drop as Reverend Border muttered the last rites whilst the coffin of Alice May was gently lowered into the ground. A tearful grief-stricken Daniel May placed a red rose on the casket of his dearly departed spouse. Cancer had taken hold only a few weeks before, but its insidiously rapid rampage had quickly reduced her to a mere skeleton. The subsequent wake was a solemn affair with the usual commiserations and words of sympathy from the small family group and well-wishers. Bereft of children and parents, May felt isolated in a world where fate had dealt him such a cruel hand. His understanding employer had granted him a week's break to help ease his pain. He knew it would be intolerable to remain in his London apartment on his own without his beloved Alice. So the next morning, he caught a Norfolk-bound train from Liverpool Street, having booked a week's sojourn at a small hotel in the remote town of Cromerton on Sea on the North Norfolk coast. A total change of scenery would surely be beneficial. The dense urbanisation soon gave way to wide expanses of open green rolling countryside dotted with small clumps of buildings passing for villages. As the train gathered pace, the images blurred into one another through the grime-covered carriage windows. A change of train at Norwich sent him further north through the wilder flat terrain of Norfolk before the emergence of a large cluster of dwellings signified the train's arrival at his destination. A short taxi ride brought him to the Colton Hotel which stood in a commanding position overlooking the main beach and promenade which seemed to stretch to infinity in either direction. Grey skies had given way to bright sunshine interspersed with large puffs of white clouds bringing with it an increase in warmth that was immediately noticeable as May stepped out onto his spacious balcony overlooking the North Sea. Relaxing on a recliner with a complimentary glass of bubbly on a bright sunny day was beginning to divert his attention from the sorrow he had endured.

*

Fortified by a further glass of vino, he took the opportunity to embrace the sea air as he ventured down onto the beach. Dinner was not for another hour, and a little light exercise should do wonders for his appetite. The sun cast elongated shadows of May and the other walkers as they crunched their way along the wide expanse of golden sands. Within a short while, he had reached the end of the bay. A rough wooden bridge brought him past a broken rock formation before he stepped down onto a beach in the next bay which was bereft of human presence. The tide was out for quite some distance and his feet compressed the wet sand close to the water's edge, leaving neat foot imprints in his wake. A glance at his watch suggested it was time to reverse his direction and head back to the hotel. As he did so, his foot caught a sharp-edged object protruding through the sand which sent him sprawling. Fortunately, no one was in the vicinity so his dignity remained intact. Cursing as he rose to his feet, he brushed off the grains of sand clinging to his garments and bent down to examine the offending item that had caused his fall to earth. Sweeping aside the sand revealed a small wooden box, about the size of a shoebox, with curious symbols surrounding a cross etched in black on the lid which was secured to the box by rusted nails. Curiosity aroused, he pulled the box from the sand, slipped it into a bag he always carried in his coat pocket and headed back to the hotel for closer examination.

Further investigation was delayed for a while whilst he consumed his gloriously tasty evening meal, washed down with a bottle of red. Recognising that May was a lone diner, a few of his fellow guests successfully engaged him in their conversations which May was open to thanks to the application of alcohol. At the conclusion of dinner, May made his way to his room feeling slightly the worse for wear yet excited at the prospect of what lay within the box. Age had clearly weakened the nails securing the lid and little effort was required to prise it off. Within lay a folded piece of parchment close to disintegration with a distinct salty odour suggesting its sojourn in the sea had been a lengthy one. The faded writing was initially hard to read but careful positioning of the table lamp enabled May to read the document.

*

"I Abraham Stark, captain of the ill-fated SS Royal Eagle, have crossed the seven seas many a time in search of the Whistle of St John. It is said to have the power to grant the recipient one wish after one use of the accursed instrument. I foolishly parted with a king's ransom to secure it from an ancient tribe of Aztec Indians in the year of our lord 1838. If you are reading this, you will have found the Whistle within the box. I implore you to destroy it, for it will bring you nothing but grief. My fatal misuse summoned an entity so evil that it laid waste to my faithful crew and it will finally take me too, as my broken ship slides under the ocean. But at least the god-forsaken thing will mercifully be lost forever. AS, 1840."

*

Not the sort of thing you want to read before retiring for the evening thought May as he nervously glanced around the room at any unusual noise. Anyway, there was nothing else within the box. Or so he thought. Further examination, however, revealed that the area which the parchment lay within was quite shallow compared to the depth of the box. Using one of the nails he had extracted from the lid, May managed to lever out a tight-fitting piece of wood to reveal a heavy object inside a worn linen bag. May let out a gasp as he pulled out a gold whistle about the size in length of a man's hand. "Rather large for a whistle," murmured May. "More like a small flute." The attention to detail was astonishing given its ancient origins. Curious symbols and inscriptions adorned the whole length. May, on his own admission, struggled with the rudiments of the English language so he had no chance of understanding what the markings were. Resisting the urge to give the whistle a blow, he read again the words on the parchment. What did Stark mean by misuse? And what was the entity that wrought such carnage?

Sleep was difficult to embrace that night as Stark's account constantly turned over in his mind. His late bleary-eyed appearance at breakfast didn't go unnoticed by his fellow guests. Wisely, he thought twice of advising them of his precious find as he was reluctant to share details of such a rare artefact given its age. But he did decide a trip to the local library might help shed some light on the whistle.

The local librarian, Mr Morden, found the object truly fascinating but was unable to translate the inscription. "I'll give Henry Bound, the resident historian at the Norwich Museum, a ring. If anybody can help you, he can," he said and reached for the phone. "Hello, Henry. I have a Mr May with me who's discovered a rare ancient artefact in the form of a gold whistle with a curious inscription which I think you will find very interesting... Okay Henry, will do," he said as he hung up. "You are in luck. Mr Bound will make himself available to you this afternoon to examine it." Morden glanced at his watch. "The 12.30 train for Norwich leaves in half an hour so if you leave now you should be in time."

"Thank you so much Mr Morden," said May,

barely containing his excitement as he promptly left to catch the train.

*

Within a couple of hours, May was at the museum and observing the historian as he peered through the glasses he had perched precariously on the end of his nose and turned the whistle over in his hands.

"Quite a unique find Mr May, with its origins going back to the 15th century I would say," said Bound.

"So what does the inscription say?" interrupted an eager May, keen to know the outcome.

Bound paused for a moment "It's in Latin as I suspected, and the message is rather cryptic," said Bound as he read aloud the inscription.

"Here I dwell to serve your needs

With one use I will grant your wish

But use me more will cost you dear.

And your remaining days may be filled with fear."

*

A sombre stance quickly replaced May's previous ebullient mood. "Sounds like a warning to me," he said, feeling rather downbeat.

"Yes, I believe it is, it seems to suggest that you

use the whistle on more than one occasion at your peril," answered Bound. "Did you bring the parchment with you?" he added.

"Yes, I did," said May, passing it over to the historian.

"Hmm," said Bound. "For whatever reason, Stark or his crew must have used the whistle more than once, leading to their inevitable doom." Collecting his thoughts, Bound resumed. "You could say the whistle represents good and evil. Still, it is a remarkable find Mr May. I'm sure the museum would reward you quite handsomely, probably in the region of £3000, if you decided to part company with it. Here is my card if you decide to take matters further."

"Thank you, Mr Bound, I will give it some thought," said May as he shook Bound's hand to say farewell.

As the train pulled out of Norwich station, May was totally oblivious to his surroundings as his mind focused on his options. Keep it and it could rise in value beyond the £3000 or sell it now. Either way, he could still make one wish. But for what? Despite his valuable acquisition he was still mourning the loss of his irreplaceable childhood sweetheart, his beloved inseparable companion for so many years.

*

Back at the hotel and conscious of the whistle's worth, May placed the box and its contents in the safe in his room. Considering that his own financial position was a little precarious, the extra cash would definitely be useful if he decided to sell. And he would have the money now. So after further thought, May rang Bound and agreed to sell for £3000. Afterwards, he freshened up and headed down to the dining room for his evening meal. The drink flowed freely as May joined his new acquaintances for an enjoyable meal with plenty of convivial conversation and laughter. But not once did he mention his recent discovery despite alcohol's best attempts to loosen his tongue.

With tiredness beginning to take its toll, he bid his fellow guests goodnight and retired to his room, moving to the balcony to enjoy a night cap. His thoughts again returned to his lost love as he watched couples strolling along the promenade, hand in hand, pausing for an embrace. And it hit May hard. In a moment of irrational thinking, his thoughts turned to the whistle. What if… Without hesitation, he took the box from the safe, sat on his bed, withdrew the whistle from its pouch and blew just once, wishing for his Alice to be with him. But within minutes, he fell into a deep asleep, the day's exhausting schedule having finally caught up with him.

*

The dawn chorus eventually woke him from his slumbers. The bright sunlight streamed through the blinds, illuminating the whole room. Then, in a fleeting moment, the sun's rays were interrupted by a human shadow on the balcony. In an instant, May raised the blinds and looked out. Nothing. Yet he was sure his eyes had not deceived him. How strange. Clearly a trick of the light he thought.

May found it impossible to recall the events of the previous evening, not surprising given his over-indulgence in the alcohol, although he hadn't woken up with a hangover. It seemed as though a brief period of his life had been permanently erased from his memory. His thoughts turned to the artefact. Quick check. Still in the safe. Why did he doubt himself?

*

Following a quick phone call to Bound, May was soon heading for the station and the next available train to Norwich with his prized possession. For some reason, he was glad he was selling the object. He was beginning to feel uncomfortable in its presence. It was as though it was taking hold of him and the fact it was so valuable made him doubt his ability to keep it safe from theft. His mood was not helped by the weather which turned damp and drizzly as he made his way onto the platform. As the train chugged into the station, it was shrouded in a blanket of mist, as though it had arrived from another dimension. As he was about to board, he observed a tall slim lady sporting a long black coat with long flowing blonde locks entering the carriage further down the platform. His dearly beloved Alice had sported an uncannily similar look. Once he had taken his seat, he expected to see the lady in the same carriage, but she was nowhere to be seen. As it was the last carriage, she would have had to pass him if she had moved through to the other carriages. But that hadn't occurred. "How very strange," thought May. But his thoughts quickly switched to keeping his valuable asset close to his person. Such was his paranoia of losing it. Within half an hour, he had alighted at Norwich station. Out of curiosity, he remained stationary just for a few minutes to see if the lady in the black coat appeared on the platform. But she never did. May cursed his overwrought imagination, dismissing the incident from his mind and making his way to the museum.

*

"It will make a very worthy addition to the exhibits we already have Mr May, I cannot thank you enough," exclaimed a highly elated Mr Bound.

"To be honest, I began to feel uneasy looking after the artefact after we met yesterday, and I'm rather relieved that the responsibility has been passed on to your good self," replied May.

"Out of interest, did you make a wish whilst it was in your possession?" enquired Bound, curious as to what the outcome was.

"Strange as it may seem, I don't recall doing so," said the slightly confused widower, desperately trying to recall the events of the night before.

"Well, would you like to do so before you hand it over?" answered the surprised historian. "I'll make myself scarce for a few minutes for you to execute said deed," added Bound.

Acknowledging Bound's discretion, May withdrew the whistle from its box and hesitated for a moment. Had he used it before he asked himself? It was still in the safe this morning so he couldn't have, could he? Satisfied that he hadn't, he closed his lips around the whistle and blew while making his wish for his Alice to be with him.

A few minutes later, Bound re-entered the room. "All done then?" he enquired. "I'd hate for you to miss out once the Whistle is in the museum's hands," added the jovial historian.

Once May had pocketed his cheque for the agreed amount, he bid Bound farewell and headed back to Norwich station for his return to Cromerton.

*

Gloomy grey skies had given way to a bright blue backdrop with the warm sun occasionally obscured by small drifts of white clouds. With the whistle away from his being and replaced by a nice fat cheque, May started to feel a lot more relaxed as he sipped a hot coffee whilst waiting for the arrival of his train. Further down the platform, his vision singled out a familiar figure – the lady in the long black coat, but this time with her hood pulled up; she was looking down the track. In a few minutes, the train came into the station and May observed the lady step into the last carriage. For a fleeting moment, her shrunken features came into view beneath the bright platform lamps and May shuddered. There was something about her physical appearance that seemed unnatural. Moments later, May climbed aboard the next carriage, moved to the last carriage and looked around. Again, the woman wasn't there. If she had walked to the next carriage, May would have seen her. Yet she was nowhere in sight. "How very odd," he thought, "it is as though she has vanished into thin air."

The veil of darkness began to sweep over the town as the packed train pulled into Cromerton station. It took a little while for the passengers to disembark and as May finally stepped off the train, he observed the lady in black on the platform, walking out of the station. His curiosity was now beginning to get the better of him and he quickened his pace to catch her up. But as he reached the exit, she was nowhere to be seen. Was he hallucinating? "Hardly," he told himself, but he couldn't dismiss her image from his mind.

*

Despite relieving himself of the whistle and receiving a financial boost, a subdued May cut a rather insular figure at dinner that evening, but with encouragement from his fellow diners, his mood soon improved, aided by a few glasses of wine. Such was his boosted wellbeing that he decided to venture out following the conclusion of dinner. He was encouraged in his decision by the steady flow of people already strolling the promenade, taking advantage of a warm late summer evening beneath a clear sky dominated by twinkling stars and a vivid full moon that illuminated the sea front like floodlights at a football stadium. May felt positivity radiating throughout his whole being as he strolled along the prom towards the brightly lit pier that protruded into the sea like a large luminous peninsula. Song and laughter echoed through the walls of the theatre as May walked up the pier to sit on a bench with glorious views across the sea to the promenade.

After a short while, May arose to walk back, just as a mist rolled in from the sea. As he started to move, he heard footsteps behind him. Turning around, his face lit up like a beacon. "Alice my lovely, you've come back to me!" exclaimed the excited man. But as she drew nearer, the enveloping mist couldn't conceal that his long-lost love was extraordinarily emaciated. Her skeletal frame was mercifully concealed by her long black coat and hood, but her hands were painfully thin and her once bright blue eyes seemed lost in the gaping sockets of a shrunken skull. Joy turned to fear and a cold sweat swept through May's being as he realised the person before him was just a pale imitation of the woman he loved. With outstretched fleshless arms, the apparition moved forwards to embrace him. May recoiled in horror and as he stepped backwards, he lost his footing on the slippery pier decking and fell over the railings into the murky heaving sea below. His pale lifeless body washed up on the shore a few days later. A distant relative handled the funeral of the late Daniel May. The cost: £3000.

THE TREASURE OF THOMAS JOHNS

Matthew Fell had led a good life if not a fulfilling one, having remained single as he crossed into his seventh decade. Now retired from his stressful but successful career as a banker, he yearned for a quieter more relaxed way of life outside the hustle and bustle of London. His busy working lifestyle in the capital had provided little time for socialising despite having a close-knit circle of friends. Flirtations with the fairer sex had occurred over the years but alas nothing that bore fruit on a permanent basis. Yet he was content with his lot and the thought of spending his remaining years in a peaceful environment couldn't be more gratifying.

Within weeks, he had found the perfect spot. A small cosy cottage in the picturesque village of Tremerton, nestled near a small bay on the East Sussex coast. Given its location, with a panoramic view overlooking the bay, Matthew was surprised that the property came in at a price somewhat cheaper than he expected compared to similar properties in the area. Still, he couldn't be happier. All the necessary amenities were within the village and there was easy access to the main routes to elsewhere. So one bright June morning, he piloted his car in a southerly direction out of the busy suburbs to a more tranquil existence on the coast. In next to no time, the open undulating countryside with its rolling fields punctuated by lines of hedges and shrubs gave way to a cluster of cottages and houses that encircled a large green space just before the contours of the land swept down into the bay. Matthew pulled up outside his diminutive 19th-century thatched roof dwelling. "Bay Cottage" – how appropriate, he thought as he paused for a moment to admire the simplicity of the design. Once he'd settled in, he couldn't wait to witness the sunsets from his south-facing garden with its glorious uninterrupted views over the sandy dunes that peppered the crescent-shaped bay beyond. It may not be heaven, but it was mighty close he murmured to himself.

*

As he consumed a welcome cup of coffee from the comfort of the wooden swing seat in his back garden, he observed that the village church stood at the edge of the bay to his left and that a distinct sandy footpath snaked down from the building, through the dunes and flowed a few feet away from the bottom of his garden before disappearing around the back of the village. Even from his vantage point and with his less-than-perfect eyesight, he observed that the structure appeared to be neglected. That would be a shame thought Matthew, who loved nothing better than visiting houses of God. Following an early supper, he retired early, the day's exertions finally catching up with him. A deep sleep brought with it the strangest of dreams.

*

Standing in his moonlit garden at the stroke of midnight, he saw a procession of four men clad in period costume emerge from the sea, walk along the beach and disappear one by one into the church at the end of the bay. A while later, the same individuals emerged from the church, running as though their lives depended on it. Each one had a look of intense fright as they scurried across the sand, glancing back in horror as a taller, more imposing figure clad in period costume and wielding a fearsome sword closed in on them. One by one, each of the pursued men was savagely cut down as they tried in vain to escape their inevitable fate. The victor removed a large bag from his final victim and headed back to the church, but not before glancing in Matthew's direction.

That image was so shocking that it woke him from

his slumbers; his bed clothes were soaked in sweat and his heart was beating so fast it felt like it might explode. Once his being began to calm down, he instinctively went to the bedroom window, drew the curtains aside and looked out over the bay. All he could see and hear was the tranquil constant motion of the white-foamed waves gently flowing up and down the beach beneath the brightest of full moons. All was a picture of serenity and peacefulness. As he was about to close the curtains, he observed that the ebb tide had revealed what appeared to be the top of a mast head just protruding above the surface of the water a few hundred yards out in the bay. "A sunken ship no doubt, which is nothing unusual," thought Matthew. "Many bays around this coastline are home to wrecks of one kind or another." In a short while, Matthew resumed his slumber, aided in no little way by a shot of whisky that helped him to relax. He slept well into the late morning only to be sharply awoken by the machine gun chatter of magpies outside his bedroom window.

*

Over his late morning breakfast, Matthew endeavoured to recall the details of his dream. Fortunately, he had a very retentive memory and the dream sequence was still vivid. The four men were clearly taking something that may or may not have belonged to their assailant. But what, and why? And what was the connection between the shipwreck and the church? Perhaps the answers may exist at the local library, and a visit to the church may also prove fruitful.

*

Matthew opted to do the latter first. Only because the warm sunny weather invited a stroll along the beach en route to the church. Taking in the fresh sea air as he crunched along the firm damp sand near the water's edge, he observed that the mast head was no longer visible, concealed again by the incoming tide. Within a short while, he was ascending the steep path up to the church with its commanding view over the bay. Pushing aside the creaking rusty metal gate revealed a site of desolation and decay. Crumbling low-slung stone walls defined the rectangular perimeter within which graves and headstones had succumbed to the ravages of time. His initial description of the structure viewed from his cottage was not far from the truth. The church was clearly a victim of coastal erosion in its severest form. Its prominent position meant it faced maximum exposure to the worst that Mother Nature could throw at it. And it showed. Shattered glass panes were evident throughout and parts of the exterior stone walls had begun to disintegrate. Why was the structure allowed to deteriorate wondered Matthew. Surprisingly, the imposing faded oak entrance doors were not fully closed and afforded sufficient space for Matthew to ease past with a little physical effort into the vestibule. The decaying inner door, however, provided a bigger challenge and required several superhuman efforts to prise it open. Fortunately for Matthew, his powerful physique came to the fore and he was able to achieve something which would have defeated a lesser human being. Passing into the nave, he walked through the thick layer of dust and detritus that coated the central aisle. He couldn't help but notice the silence within, save for the occasional sound of scurrying small creatures. It was as though he'd stepped back in time.

*

It was clearly evident that the building had not seen a service for many a year and its dilapidated state was sad to see. Stepping up into the quire and then up to the altar, he noticed that a few feet behind it was a narrow opening with stone steps that spiralled down under the church. Curiosity held sway over caution and Matthew descended the winding stone steps, eager to investigate. Even in the full light of day, the tall stained-glass windows afforded restricted light in that area of the church. Fortunately, he had a torch in his coat to illuminate the way. Within seconds, he'd reached yet another door but this one failed to yield despite Matthew's best efforts. He realised that the door had an internal lock which was clearly thwarting his efforts. How annoying. But as he turned round to exit, his elbow struck a loose brick that fell to the floor just missing his feet on its descent. In the exposed recess, his torch beam picked out a small drawstring cloth bag. Within which was a corroded key that, much to Matthew's delight, opened the door.

It led into a small damp chamber; the obnoxious fetid odour of the room nearly took Matthew's breath away. Dominating the room was an imposing grey oak tomb. Inscribed on the lid was the following: "Captain Thomas Johns, saviour of our village". Eager to see what lay inside, Matthew slid the dirt-encrusted cover to one side. As he did so, he felt an invisible presence brush past him from within the coffin. For a brief moment, he froze, for on the inside lay a skeleton clad in a typical pirate outfit of the 18th century. The jaws were wide open and lined with broken teeth and the skull seemed to glare at Matthew through unseen eyes. He found its mocking stance quite unnerving. What then caught Matthew's eye was a shabby bag clasped tightly to the occupant's chest by its long spindly fingers. Overcome with an overwhelming need to discover what was in the bag, Matthew didn't stop to consider the wisdom of his actions but proceeded to pull the bag from Johns' grisly grip. This was not achieved without some physical force – its owner was clearly reluctant to relinquish his hold on his possessions! The weight nearly caught Matthew unawares as he lowered it to the floor. On opening the bag, his expression turned to one of amazement for within it was a hoard of gold coins. They could be worth a fortune was Matthew's first reaction but this was tempered by the fact that removal of said items would constitute theft, an act that Matthew had never undertaken in his life, being a god-fearing individual. Not to mention the fate of the men in his dream who had tried to undertake the same deed. So despite the initial temptation, he returned the bag and its contents to its previous position and slid back the coffin top. He then closed and locked the chamber door, returned the key to its original location, replaced the stone and exited the church, ensuring the outer doors were in the same positions as he found them, but not before sweeping aside his footprints as he left, thus removing all evidence of his entry.

*

The sun was beginning to disappear beyond the horizon as Matthew made his way back to his cottage, retracing the route he had taken earlier. The fading rays of the sun cast long shadows across the damp sand, artificially increasing his size to that of a giant. But Matthew was taking little interest in his surroundings because his mind was totally focused on the discovery within the depths of the church as he trudged along the twisting sandy path between the dunes back to his cottage. As he opened the gate to his back garden, he observed that the swing seat was gently swaying to and fro although there was no wind to provide the movement. "How strange," thought Matthew. But distraction was short-lived as his mind swiftly turned to his next objective – a visit to the library. Pausing briefly to consume a midday lunch, he was soon on his way to Liverton to continue with his quest. It was good that patience was one of Matthew's virtues because the librarian seemed to take an age to track down the early history of the village.

"Apologies for the delay but the tome had been misplaced, necessitating a time-consuming search," said the librarian who then proceeded to brush off the layers of dust suggesting its tenure untouched had been a lengthy one. Matthew was surprised at the size and weight of the faded leather-bound opus.

Anticipating his reaction, the librarian commented, "Quite a weight isn't it?"

"Yes, surprisingly so," said Matthew. "Is it possible to take it home on loan please?" he asked. "I only live a few miles away in Tremerton and I would be happy to make a donation to the library's charity."

"I see no reason why not, it's not exactly in demand," quipped the librarian. "Just leave your address and phone number," he added.

Within a short while an elated Matthew was back home, eager to explore the contents of his new acquisition.

*

On each turn of the yellowing pages, the history of the village began to unfold. The first few inhabitants had moved in shortly after the Norman conquest in 1066 and the church was built shortly thereafter. For a while the community had thrived, but a mysterious plague decimated the village and it was abandoned for many years until the late 17th century.

Outsiders then began to drift back into the village, drawn by the offer of work at nearby farms which began to thrive. The bay was an ideal temporary landing spot for pirate ships to anchor and secure provisions before continuing their nefarious ways. But one particular individual, Captain Thomas Johns of the Black Wolf, bucked the trend and opted to forgo his previous lifestyle and settle in the village. Although the source of his wealth was clearly questionable, the village began to thrive under his guidance and wealth.

Unfortunately, this harmonious state of affairs didn't last. A number of years later, the Black Wolf returned to the bay, now captained by the former first mate Abram Marley. Marley and his crew had fallen on hard times having squandered their share of their ill-gotten gains and, knowing that Johns had taken a sizeable fortune when he forsook his piracy ways, they were hoping to find their former captain in a charitable mood. Johns was not without compassion and agreed to meet Marley on the beach near the church late one stormy night, bringing with him a bag of gold coins to aid his former colleagues' plight. But Marley was dissatisfied with the amount on offer and a heated argument ensued. Marley and his three accomplices then unleashed a frenzied attack on Johns, killing him instantly, such was the ferocity of the onslaught. Following that terrible deed, the four assassins, convinced that further coins lay within the church, searched the building but to no avail. Conscious of the increasing storm, the four men returned to the Black Wolf, complete with the bag of Spanish gold coins offered by the late Thomas Johns. Although Marley and his crew were seasoned mariners, the storm was so ferocious that, despite their considerable experience, they couldn't prevent the ship smashing against the rocks beneath the raging sea and sinking within minutes, drowning all on board. It was as though the storm had exacted a revenge on the four murderers.

The following day, calmer conditions prevailed and the beach was strewn with corpses and detritus from the Black Wolf, including the bag of gold coins and the decimated body of the late Thomas Johns. The incident shocked the locals so much that Johns was given a funeral befitting a man who had given so much to the village. His body was subsequently buried in a secret chamber deep within the church, together with the remains of his monetary fortune. Unfortunately, in later years the church fell into disrepair as rumours began to circulate that the ghost of Thomas Johns roamed the church and graveyard late at night. The exodus of worshippers began when Jonah Tree, a regular patron, vowed never to return after seeing a ghostly apparition moving down the aisle. But what really scared him was when the ghost briefly glanced in his direction before disappearing behind the altar. Tree could never bring himself to describe what he saw. Subsequent sightings by other church goers were enough to deter even the most ardent attendee. So the church was abandoned for good.

Despite flicking through numerous subsequent pages, Matthew was unable to track down any relevant further entries. Just as he was closing the book, the phone began to ring.

"Hello Matt my old friend, how are you?"

"Keeping well Tom, it's been a while," replied a surprised Matthew.

"Listen Matt, I was thinking of coming down to see you in your new abode when it's convenient," said an excited Tom.

"Sounds like a great idea Tom, how about this coming weekend?"

"Great, we'll see you this coming Friday for a good catch up."

Tom and Matthew were old school friends who had kept in touch through the years although their career paths had taken them in different directions. Whilst Matthew was successful in his chosen career, Tom could never hold a job down for long and was financially less solvent than his friend. But the two had forged a special bond of friendship which remained undiminished despite the passage of time.

*

Later that day, Matthew returned the book to the library at Liverton.

"Fascinating story of Tremerton church, but was the haunting the real reason for its abandonment?" he enquired.

"Well, some descendants of those who lived in Tremerton still believe the spirit of Thomas Johns exists but the real reason was coastal erosion," replied the librarian. "Because the church was built so close to the beach the foundations have been weakened by the constant battering of the onshore winds and fierce storms so any restoration work would in the long run be futile, and at some point in time what remains of it will disappear into the sea along with Johns and his fortune."

"How sad," replied Matthew in a reflective mood. "Couldn't the rest of Johns' wealth have been used to support the village?" he added curiously.

"Yes it could but Johns had already used a large part of his fortune to help the village and his will made it clear he was to be buried with what remained."

"Hmm, how interesting," said Matthew, thanking the librarian for the loan of the book as he left the library.

*

On the way home, Matthew's thoughts returned to that nightmarish dream in which Johns had chillingly exacted due retribution on those who had stolen his fortune. Was it a coincidence that the four seafarers who cut down their captain all those years ago also met an untimely end? Matthew's initial reaction was to leave well alone. But if the church disappeared into the sea, then Johns' fortune would be lost forever. Wouldn't that be a tragic waste? If the money was put to good use, surely the late Thomas Johns would approve?

*

Sleep was not easy to come by that night as his mind was constantly in turmoil over the course of action to take. It was late the following morning before Matthew emerged from his slumbers, woken by the sound of his phone.

"Hello Matt, Tom here. I should be with you late this afternoon."

"Ok Tom, look forward to seeing you later," replied Matthew, doing his best to be sociable despite his drowsy condition.

In no time at all, Matthew had secured provisions from the local shops and made the spare room comfortable for his friend's forthcoming arrival. By mid-afternoon, tasks completed, Matthew retired to the back garden to take in the glorious views across the bay. The afternoon sun swept its intermittent rays, created by rolling isolated clouds, across the bay, vividly illuminating the church as it began to move towards the west. A glass of chilled white wine created a sublime feeling of total relaxation. Within minutes, Matthew heard the crunch of car wheels on the gravel driveway. Tom had arrived.

"Good to see you old friend," said Tom as Matthew moved forwards to embrace him.

"It's been too long Tom," replied Matthew. "Please come in, fancy a glass of vino before dinner?"

"Perfect," said Tom.

Drinks in hand, Matthew guided his friend to the comfortable seating in his garden.

"Wow what a marvellous view!" exclaimed Tom. "I can see why you wanted to retire here," he added.

"Yes, I fell in love with it immediately on first viewing and the location is peaceful too," said his host.

"Looks like the church has seen better days though – and is that a ship's mast I can see out to sea?" asked Tom as he surveyed the scenery before him.

"Right on both observations my friend," Matthew replied, impressed that Tom had such a keen eye for detail. "There is an interesting tale that connects the two." The look on Tom's face suggested that his friend was eager to know more. "It was an awful dream I had on my first night here which ignited my interest," Matthew said, before explaining his nightmare and subsequent events.

Tom broke the temporary silence that followed the conclusion of Matthew's tale. "It does seem a shame that the gold coins could be lost forever," he said wistfully. "In today's money, they must be worth a small fortune," he added.

"I agree Tom, my mind has been in constant turmoil over what to do," said Matthew. "I think dinner is ready," he added, seemingly keen to change the subject.

Dinner passed by in a flurry as the friends exchanged tales of events that had occurred in their lives since they had last met; the conversation flowed as freely as the wine.

"Shame about your accountancy practice folding Tom," said Matthew as the conversation switched to his friend's misfortunes in business.

"Yes, a few bad clients and ridiculously high rents put paid to that business," said Tom. "I'm doing some book-keeping now; the money's not great but I'll survive and the job's permanent so can't complain," he added.

Sensing his friend was experiencing a sombre mood, Matthew suggested they take a walk along the beach and up to the church to take advantage of the seemingly endless daylight before retiring for the evening.

"Great idea Matt!" exclaimed Tom, keen to escape his morose mood.

"I've given it a lot of thought and it does seem a travesty to let the gold coins disappear into the sea forever when they could be sold and the proceeds used to help the village prosper," said Matthew as they trundled towards the church.

"Can't help but agree Matt, it would be such a waste."

"Then we will remove them for a greater good," replied Matthew, believing he had made the right decision.

*

A gentle warm breeze brushed their faces as the two men climbed the winding sandy path up to the church. The church's dilapidated state was clearly evident as they approached the entrance gate.

"Shame it's been allowed to go to rack and ruin," sighed Tom. "Must have been impressive in its heyday," he added.

"Yes, the images of it then are quite spectacular," Matthew replied. "I was lucky to locate the key as you well know, otherwise I would never have gained access to the chamber," he added.

There was no evidence of visits by others since Matthew's previous trip as they made their way to the chamber under the church.

"Quite cold down here don't you think Matt?" said a shivering Tom.

"Never noticed the coolness before but you're right," replied Matthew as he slid the oak lid off the coffin to reveal the skeletal remains of its occupant who appeared to take on a more sinister appearance in the fading light.

"Wouldn't want to meet him down a dark alley," jested Tom as his attention was drawn to the bag in the owner's hands.

"Yes, not the most appealing of individuals but what is in the bag definitely is," replied Matthew as he once again withdrew the linen bag from the grasping skeletal hand.

"Wow it's quite heavy Matt, although the bag is quite modest in size," exclaimed Tom.

"Exactly my reaction when I first took hold of it," replied Matt. "I expect a history museum would offer quite a tidy sum for these. I counted about 150 of them, hence the weight," he added.

Both men ensured everything was as before as they carefully exited the church, checking there was nobody in the vicinity as they made their way back along the footpath towards the rear of the sand dunes, the bag hidden from sight inside Matthew's coat…

*

Alan Meads was taking his usual evening walk along the top of the cliffs when he observed a tall man emerge from the church and advance at pace along the beach. As far as he was aware, the church was completely derelict and locked to all visitors. Where had this person come from? Much further along, he could see two men passing behind the tall sand dunes that dominated the bay. Curiosity triggered Meads to remove the small binoculars from his coat pocket to take a closer look at the first person. A look of fright crossed his features as he observed a being so hideously thin that he couldn't believe it was alive grasping in its tightly clenched right hand, or more accurately its long bony claw, a long knife or sword. Its gaunt bloodless face was partially concealed by a black hood, but what was visible – a grinning eyeless skull – nearly made Meads drop his binoculars. The entity was clearly in pursuit of the two men ahead of him and whilst Meads wouldn't consider himself the bravest of individuals, he felt an overwhelming desire to warn those in peril.

Throwing caution to the wind, he swiftly changed direction and took the shortest route over the dunes as fast as his legs would carry him As he ascended the first dune, terrifying screams assaulted his eardrums. A chilling sensation crept over Meads as he sensed his arrival would be in vain. His worst fears were founded – as he descended the steep dune his eyes caught sight of two bodies spread-eagled on the path, their bodies horribly mutilated. And in the distance, he saw the black-hooded man running back towards the church carrying a cloth bag. The awful scene proved too much for Meads and he passed out at the bottom of the dunes.

*

A vigorous shake of his shoulder aroused Meads from his deep state of unconsciousness. His face was a ghastly white.

"Looks like you've seen a ghost my friend," said a tall emaciated elderly man clad in black. "Another few feet and the tide would have swept you out to sea."

Meads shakily climbed to his feet, profusely shaking his saviour's unnaturally thin cold hand in gratitude as he observed that the advancing waves were perilously close to where he had fallen. Meads then noticed that there was no sign of the slain bodies anywhere, presumably swallowed up by the advancing sea.

"May I buy you a drink at the Red Wolf as a thank you?" asked Meads.

"Well that's kind of you," answered the old man, whose gaunt features made Meads feel a shade uneasy.

Once in the pub, beers in hand, Meads was keen to tell his tale.

The old man seemed surprisingly unmoved by Meads' unpleasant experience. "Well I've lived here a very long time and there have been rumours of incidents in the distant past when ill-advised folk tried to steal a man's fortune only to meet an untimely end," said the old timer. "Sounds as though greed reared its ugly head yet again," he wistfully added.

"But the manner in which they died?" replied Meads.

"I'm sure in time the incident will fade from your memory," said the old man, seemingly avoiding a more appropriate answer and with that, the two men said their goodbyes and went their separate ways.

As they left the pub, Meads observed the man turn down an overgrown footpath that led to the old church. Believing that there were no dwellings in that direction, Meads was driven by curiosity to follow him at a discreet distance. The old man was walking up towards the churchyard gate when a startled animal in a nearby hedge momentarily broke Meads' attention and when he glanced back, the man was nowhere to be seen. "How very strange," thought Meads, who never saw the man again.

WETHERING FOREST

Patience was not one of Isaac Boden's greatest virtues and what little he had was being tested as he waited for his wife to pick up her phone only for the connection to fail again. No signal. "Great," murmured Boden. Stranded on a narrow back road in the middle of Wethering Forest miles from anywhere with a broken-down car didn't exactly fill him with joy. With his negligible knowledge of automobiles he knew that to raise the bonnet to try and identify the source of failure would be an utter waste of time. And to make matters even worse, it had started to rain. Fortunately, he did have the forethought to carry with him a raincoat and a brolly the size of a parachute. It was clear that to remain in his car in the vain hope of imminent rescue in such a desolate place was inadvisable so without hesitation, he abandoned his stricken vehicle and ventured up the road in the direction he was going.

*

It was early afternoon on a Friday at the end of October yet the low-slung rain clouds and the tall tightly packed trees that seemed to stretch interminably into the heavens on either side of the road suggested nightfall was imminent. As he strode purposefully up the ever-twisting asphalt, he remained confident that he would soon encounter help. He glanced at his watch – nearly an hour had passed since he left his vehicle and still no sign of life. The light of day soon gave way to the enveloping blanket of darkness. But just as he was beginning to lose the will to live, he saw in the distance the headlamps of a car increasing in size as it drew closer. Within a few minutes, the vehicle screeched to a halt, the driver recognising the walker's plight.

*

Boden was well aware that his Ford Escort was not the last word in modernity, but the car before him made his vehicle look positively state of the art. It reminded him of the cars driven by American gangsters during the prohibition years in the 1920s and its owner didn't look much younger either. His distinctive attire was difficult to ignore. Or perhaps it was a trick of the light.

"Good evening, may I offer you a lift?" said the well-spoken driver. His tone suggested a willingness to help.

"That's very kind of you, my car broke down a few miles down the road as I was heading for Beacon Town," replied Boden, pleasantly relieved.

"Well that's some miles away and the garage will be closed. I live close by, you are quite welcome to stay overnight at our house and I'll arrange for the garage to attend to your car tomorrow. The name's Gerald Mellish."

"Isaac Boden," came the natural response. With no other option, Boden gladly accepted the invitation although he couldn't help feeling a little apprehensive about staying with a complete stranger. Once inside his saviour's ancient car, his first impressions of the vehicle were reinforced. A spindly steering wheel the size of a satellite dish dominated the dated dashboard, it had a column gear change and whilst the leather seats were comfortable, the absence of seatbelts certainly betrayed the car's age. A classic car no doubt but unlikely to be his main mode of transport or so Boden thought. After a mile or so, a faded worn wooden sign appeared on the left: "… Manor" was all that could be seen – ivy obscured the first part of the name. A wide dirt track snaked its way through a dense mass of tall trees before opening up onto a circular pebbled drive in front of an imposing three-storey Victorian mansion.

*

"Edith, my sister, will be preparing dinner soon. I'm sure there will be more than enough for another," said Mellish with a smile as he brought his car to an abrupt halt outside the imposing oak entrance door. As Boden stepped into the hallway, he felt he had stepped back in time. The furnishings and decor smacked of early pre-war Britain.

Mellish ushered Boden into the vast dimly lit living room adorned with huge pictures and dominated by an imposing brick fireplace with a fire roaring in the hearth. It seemed a bit excessive for the time of year but the room definitely required some warmth. As he offered his guest one of the sumptuous large leather armchairs close to the fireplace, he asked Boden if he would like a cup of tea.

"That would be great," Boden replied. "I am feeling rather parched," he added.

Within a short while, Mellish returned to the living room accompanied by his sister carrying an ornate silver tray with three exquisite china cups, a teapot and some biscuits.

"Pleased to meet you Mr Boden, I understand that you had a misfortune with your car."

"Unfortunately, Miss Mellish," replied Boden,

observing that her attire was similar to that of her sibling. "The workings of a car have always been a mystery to me."

"Same here old boy," chipped in Mellish. "Marvellous invention but a bugger when they go wrong," he jested. "Old George down at Masons Motors will sort you out."

Pausing to take a drink of his welcome brew, Boden could not help but notice the uncanny physical similarities between brother and sister. "Are you..."

"Twins?" said Mellish, easily anticipating Boden's line of questioning. "Correct Mr Boden, we were both launched into the world at the same time with only our sexes telling us apart," came another jocular response.

Boden's inquisitive nature came to the fore. "Have you both lived here long?" he enquired.

"Since we were born nearly eight decades ago," responded Mellish. "Our grandparents built this place at the turn of the century," he added.

"They did a grand job," said Boden as his eyes swept around the room, admiring the enviable attention to detail. What did catch his attention was the large family portrait mounted above the fireplace. "Lovely picture," he added.

"Thank you," replied Mellish, "very striking isn't it?"

"Absolutely," said Boden. "Almost true to life."

Boden was looking at a scene of a man and a woman in classic smart Edwardian attire with what appeared to be their four offspring sitting down in front of them. Three girls and a boy. The imposing fireplace in the background provided the perfect backdrop.

"My grandfather was a keen artist in his time. This features our parents, Edith, myself and our sisters Matilda and Annabel. Annabel lives abroad now and Matilda sadly died from a brain tumour a few years ago."

"Very sorry to hear that," said Boden sympathetically. "You must miss her terribly."

"To be honest, we still can't believe she's gone," interjected Edith. "The cancer took her very quickly," she added.

A few minutes' silence ensued before Edith signalled dinner was ready.

*

Further convivial conversation ensued whilst the threesome tucked into a roast chicken dinner.

"Absolutely lovely dinner, Miss Mellish," said Boden as he washed down his meal with a final glass of red wine.

"Glad you enjoyed it Mr Boden, Edith is a wonderful cook."

Following the conclusion of dinner, coffee was served back in the living room where further exchanges of conversation passed the time. The imposing grandfather clock struck 11pm with a resounding chime that seemed to echo throughout the building.

"Ah, bedtime beckons," said Mellish. "Edith will show you to your room," he added as he glanced in her direction.

*

"We've given you the room overlooking the rear garden," said Edith as they ascended the staircase to the upper floor. "I'm sure you will approve of the view," she added.

And she was right. Boden stood in front of the large window admiring the garden which was intensely illuminated by a vivid full moon. The vast expanse of sloping lawn was dominated by a large oak tree whose girth suggested it had been present for many a year. Its long misshapen limbs seemed to reach up into the heavens and spread out into the surrounding countryside. Its abundant foliage seemed to blot out the sky. At the base, surrounded by overgrown grass, a wooden bench faced the Mellish mansion. But what hypnotised Boden's attention was the presence of a woman clad in a long hooded blue cloak with flowing gold hair perched on the bench. Her piercing eyes seemed to unnaturally penetrate the artificial light as she gazed in Boden's direction.

A while later, footsteps along the hallway broke his attention. Mellish's panicked voice broke the silence. "She's out again, did you not lock the door?"

"Of course I did Gerald, I always do," replied his sister nervously.

The voices faded away as Boden's curiosity was aroused as to who "she" was. And why was her door locked? Returning his view to the garden, he observed the woman slowly rise from the bench and begin to walk back to the house. But as she drew closer, a cold shiver spread over his being as her features became more defined. One arm was significantly shorter than the other with long claws for hands and her shambling gait suggested a similar affliction affected the lower limbs. Her head seemed unusually large with bulbous steely blue eyes that protruded unnaturally from her skull. But it was the evil grin that continued to fix its gaze on Boden as she entered the house that nearly made him pass out. Just about maintaining his composure, he closed the curtains as a hideous scream filtered through into his room. Fearing the worst for his elderly hosts, Boden burst into the hallway to witness the malformed woman bending over the writhing body of Edith Mellish, her claw-like hands tightly gripping her neck, causing it to turn a deep shade of purple. Without hesitation, Boden pulled the creature away and pinned her arms behind her back, holding her down on the floor.

"Thank you Mr Boden," said Miss Mellish as she struggled to get her breath back.

At that moment, a panic-stricken Mellish appeared. Fixing a sturdy pair of handcuffs to the wriggling creature cowering beneath Mr Boden, he frogmarched her up to the top floor and locked her in her room.

*

"I think we all need a stiff drink after that, let's adjourn to the living room," said Mellish, trying to keep his composure and making sure that Edith had recovered from her ordeal. "Can't thank you enough Mr Boden," said a grateful Mellish. "Your intervention was timely." After pausing for breath, Mellish continued. "Edith and I have not been entirely truthful about the extent of our family. That person you had the misfortune to encounter is our youngest sister, Agnes.

"So there were five of you?" interrupted Boden.

"Yes, she was born with such awful deformities that the doctors said it would be kinder to let her die, but our parents would hear nothing of it and were determined to bring her up. Unfortunately, as she grew older, she was prone to bouts of schizophrenia and could not speak or hear."

"Oh dear, it seems her life was doomed from the moment she was born," said Boden.

"Yes, unfortunately so," replied Mellish. "But our parents were determined that she should have a normal life even though most of the time she was locked in her room, which fortunately is spacious enough for her needs. She was allowed out into the garden only if supervised as socialising is clearly off the agenda given her physical appearance. When our parents died, it was left up to us siblings to look after her. Edith and I have had that unenviable task for a number of years now," he added.

"It can't be easy for either of you given your age," suggested Boden.

"That's true, but she is our flesh and blood and we couldn't bear to send her to a sanatorium," sighed Mellish.

*

A period of quiet followed before the imposing grandfather clock sent out resounding chimes.

"All Hallows Eve!" exclaimed Mellish. "The night of the dead is upon us."

Boden chose to ignore that remark as the ramblings of an elderly man, not recognising it significance. It was well past midnight when the threesome retired for a second time.

The day's exertions finally caught up with Boden and he fell into a deep sleep. The peacefulness of his surroundings only emphasised the intensity of the dawn chorus as the early morning sun pierced the thinly lined curtains to illuminate the room; the combination of both aroused him from his slumbers. His hosts were already engaged in breakfast as Boden ventured downstairs into the kitchen.

"Good morning Isaac, I trust you eventually got some sleep," said Mellish.

"Better than I thought," replied Boden.

"That's good considering the unfortunate incident that occurred last night," said a sheepish Mellish.

Following a hearty meal, Boden said his farewell to Edith Mellish as he climbed into her brother's ancient machine for the journey to Beacon Town.

"Dammit," said Mellish, "fuel is rather low, but should be enough to get us there," he added as he fired up the engine.

After a number of miles, the car started to falter and eventually ground to a halt. Right at the very edge of the wood. It was as though the vehicle refused to go any farther. Judgement was clearly not one of Mellish's greatest assets thought Boden.

"Is the town far from here?" said the frustrated passenger.

"Thankfully it's only mile away," replied the embarrassed driver, cursing his car under his breath.

"Look Gerald, if you stay with the car, I will walk into town to Masons Motors to seek assistance."

"Great idea," responded Mellish as Boden strode purposefully along the undulating road down into the town. Luckily, the route was downhill which assisted Boden in his progress as did the clement weather. But as time passed, Boden was unconvinced that the town was just a mile away. More than double that distance thought the exhausted walker as he entered the town. Within a few hundred yards, he spotted Masons Motors. Salvation at last said Boden to himself.

*

Conveying his recent misfortune and experiences to the proprietor Henry Mason sparked the kind of look which suggested Boden had lost his sanity. "Well I wouldn't be rude enough to suggest what you experienced didn't happen, but my late father who started this garage years ago often did business for the Mellish family in the years prior to the war. But one night during 1940, a German bomber targeting a munitions factory near here released its bomb load to soon and it obliterated part of the forest including Mellish Manor. All the occupants – mother, father and four or five children – died instantly. Their bodies were never found. But over the years, rumours began to spread that the forest was haunted. Tourists walking through the wood sometimes reported sightings of adults and children dressed in pre-war clothing. The only survivor of that tragic event was the youngest daughter, disfigured since birth, who had been committed to an asylum just before the war broke out. She was later hanged for stabbing one of the care nurses to death."

"Well I know what I witnessed," said a bewildered Boden.

"I'm not questioning what you saw," replied Mason. "I've got the recovery truck outside, let's get your car back on the road," he added.

With that, the two men climbed aboard and headed back to the forest.

Boden was still finding it difficult to assimilate what he had just been told. But as they entered the vast wood, Mellish's vehicle was nowhere to be seen. The tall trees were so tightly packed together that they seemed to shut out the sky as the vehicle headed deeper into the wood. On the left, a rotten signpost with the words "Mellish Manor" caught Boden's eye.

"The old track still exists, and parts of the manor ruins are still visible beneath the vegetation," said Mason as they swept past.

Within minutes, Boden's car came into view.

"Just as I thought, a blocked fuel filter," said Mason as he bent down to examine the engine. Within next to no time, Mason had Boden's car purring like a pussycat. A grateful Boden insisted on payment despite Mason's initial reluctance to accept and piloted his vehicle down the road and out of the forest. He pulled into a lay-by just beyond and successfully made contact with his better half much to her relief. He never mentioned the recent incidents. She would never believe him. But Isaac Boden knew that when he entered Wethering Forest for a brief period in his life, he had stepped back in time to another life, another world. An experience which stayed with him for the rest of his life.

THE BRIDGE

Roger Cavell's job as a travelling salesman took him across vast areas of the UK. And he loved it. He thrived on exploring hitherto unknown regions which he had never heard of let alone seen. Sure there were incidents when customers were not the most endearing of individuals, but generally speaking, there were few issues and Cavell considered himself fortunate to be in such a satisfying occupation One of his favourite haunts was the Western Downs in South Devon. His next port of call was to a regular customer who resided on the edge of this sprawling mass of green undulating terrain, not dissimilar to the roller-coaster configurations popular at pleasure parks.

It was mid-winter and the cloak of darkness was already starting to descend when Cavell, threading his way along the ever-familiar A256 through the vast expanses of rolling farmland, spotted the dreaded "Road Closed" sign mounted on the left-hand side of the road and suggesting the driver exit at the next road. From previous unforgettable experiences, he knew this was likely to send him on an unfamiliar and longer route, adding time to his journey and thus delaying his next appointment. An unrepeatable expletive emerged from his lips as he completed the manoeuvre at the next junction. This carried him onto a much narrower road with passing places on either side with clusters of weeds bursting through the crumbling tarmac. Given its state, Cavell quickly concluded that this stretch of road hadn't seen a motor vehicle for quite some time.

The increasing blanket of night engulfed the landscape quicker than he had expected. Cavell reduced his speed significantly as he continued to negotiate the ever-narrowing twisting road in the rapidly gathering gloom. Recognising that he was not going to reach his client in time, he pulled to the side of the road to make a call on his mobile. No signal. Great. That's all he needed. A further expletive-ridden outburst followed which did little to improve his mood. A glance at his A-to-Z map failed to identify the existence of any road in the vicinity he now unfortunately found himself in. "How strange is that," thought Cavell. Yet this distinctive road clearly led somewhere. Convinced that a place of some kind would surely emerge at some point, Cavell soldiered on as night finally descended.

After a mile or so, his headlamps picked up a signposted fork in the road. The reassurance that directions to a familiar place or road were imminent lightened his mood as he brought his vehicle to a halt at the fork. His watch showed midnight had arrived. Cavell couldn't believe he'd been on the road that long. An upward glance at the writing scrawled on the two worn wooden signs soon brought his mood back down. The left one indicated The Bridge and the other The Quarry. Cavell opted for the route to the bridge, hoping the road would continue beyond that point although he wasn't holding his breath.

After a few more miles, he felt the need to pull into a small clearing adjacent to the road to answer the call of nature. The full moon lit up the open countryside so brightly you could be forgiven for thinking daylight had arrived early. To his left, overgrown wasteland inclined gradually to a flat peak where Cavell could just make out the structure of a small cottage partially hidden by a cluster of tall shrubs. A light was illuminating a small window, suggesting habitation within. If so, the occupant could hopefully point Cavell in the right direction towards his destination. Hopes buoyed by this prospect, he fired up his engine and moved off in search of a track of some kind leading up to the dwelling, as there was no obvious route from where he was currently parked.

After a few hundred yards, he spotted a rough

track that snaked its way towards the cottage. Not wide enough for a car but just about traversable by foot. A signpost with "Bridge Cottage" etched on the rotting wood was visible in the car's headlights. Stepping out of his car, he could hear the sound of running water, suggesting that the bridge was perhaps close at hand. Cavell was tempted to drive on but the advice of a local was clearly a better option. The cool air was still and pure, punctuated only by the odour of the resident vegetation as he crunched up the path, a mixture of shingle and weed. After a few minutes, Cavell came upon a clearing in which a diminutive thatched cottage resided. A stream of light from the small square windows helped to supplement the moon-drenched landscape as he advanced to the front door. It took several firm knocks to elicit a response from within.

"Who's there?" enquired the resident, whose tone suggested he was of an advanced age.

"Hello, name's Roger Cavell, I'm a business traveller who's lost his way. I'm seeking advice on how to get back on the main road."

A long pause ensued before the sound of several door bolts sliding back accosted Cavell's ears. Seemed rather extreme thought Cavell. As the door slowly creaked open, a waft of nauseous stale air briefly assaulted his nostrils as a gaunt elderly man sporting clothing of a bygone era filled the entrance. His long white locks cascaded down to his shoulders but there was an alertness in his piercing blue eyes.

"Sorry to have troubled you Mr…"

"Luther Stone," came the sharp reply. "Don't have many people come this way, only those who get lost. Please come in," chortled the old man as he ushered Cavell into his dwelling, seeing that his guest didn't pose a threat. Cavell was initially reluctant to enter but felt it was rude to decline, especially since he was seeking the man's help and it did seem he was longing for some company. Taking a seat close to the open fire in the living room as indicated by his host, Cavell noticed that the air within didn't seem quite as obnoxious as it was outside – or maybe he was just getting used to it.

"Fancy a cuppa? I was just making a brew," said Stone. As he moved into the kitchen to prepare the beverage, Cavell surveyed his surroundings. Much of the furnishings and decor were easily a few decades old. It was as though Cavell had stepped way back in time. What did surprise Cavell was the number of robust bolts on the door. He counted four. Most people have one or two at the most – why four?

When Stone returned with the tea, Cavell found it difficult to resist asking the obvious question. His host took a deep breath, glanced at the door and paused for a moment before responding.

"Well some years ago, I lived in Hamerton, a village close by where my best friend Abel Tomkins and I grew up together. We went to the same school and worked together on the same farm. We were to some extent inseparable, having the same interests etc. Then a family moved into the village and took over the local store. Their oldest daughter, Rose Manning, worked behind the counter and attracted a lot of male interest, especially from Abel who became besotted with her. In next to no time, their whirlwind romance led to an engagement. I became rather embittered as I saw less and less of my friend who found every excuse to be with her and not with me. Hatred overtook friendship and I began to curse the day Rose moved into the village.

"Abel was a keen motorcyclist and one of his favourite bike rides was Hamerton to Clapton on the route via the old stone bridge nearby. But one fateful rainy night, his bike skidded and crashed into the bridge wall. The impact flung Abel and Rose into the raging river, but not before Abel hit the wall first, killing him outright. Rose was eventually rescued from the river by a passer-by but never fully recovered from her injuries physically and mentally. And up to the day she died, she was convinced I was the instigator of Abel's demise due to my obvious jealousy. In one of her outbursts, she claimed that I had sabotaged the bike. I failed miserably to convince her that I had nothing to do with that terrible accident. So much so that on her deathbed she swore that, come the witching hour, I would pay for my sins. Well that was 50 years ago and I'm still here," he chortled.

"That's a fascinating tale – but it still doesn't explain the four bolts," commented his curious guest.

"Well there have been occasions in the past when the door has had to withstand pressure on it from an unknown origin, which may or may not be related to the above incident. It sounds crazy but it's true. I don't fear the supernatural, but I do believe it exists."

"So what is the witching hour?" enquired Cavell, his curiosity now somewhat aroused.

"It's when the undead – ghosts, demons and other creatures of the night – are at their most active during the hour after midnight," replied Stone, glancing out of the window as the moon rose higher in the sky, brilliantly illuminating the rolling fields beyond. "Particularly on a night such as this," he added.

"Wow, that is really creepy!" exclaimed Cavell whilst looking at his watch. 12.40am. "Would you like me to stay, just in case?" added Cavell.

"I appreciate your gesture but I'll be fine," said Stone. "I've survived many a year before tonight," he added with a wry smile. "Besides there's only a few minutes to go before the hour passes," he further added, looking up at a grandfather clock outside Cavell's line of vision.

"I expect you would like to be on your way Mr Cavell," said Stone, sensing his guest's next intention. "If you take the route over the bridge, it will bring you to a T-junction. Turn right there and you should be in familiar territory."

"Thank you for your hospitality," replied Cavell as they shook hands and said their goodbyes. Stepping out into the cool still air of the night, Cavell could hear a pin drop, such was the tranquillity and peacefulness that encompassed the surrounding countryside as he made his way back down the winding track. Glancing back, he saw Stone wave at him from outside his door and Cavell did likewise before Stone re-entered his home. To Cavell's left, down the slope of the hill, he could just make out the outline of a grey stone bridge that crossed a wide stream that snaked its way a few hundred yards from the rear of Stone's cottage. He hadn't noticed this on his ascent due to a cluster of shrubs that thwarted his view. As he turned his attention back to the route to his car, he heard the distinctive sound of splashing water above the sound of the slow-moving stream. Instinctively he stopped in his tracks and turned to locate the source. His face turned a deathly white and his whole being began to tremble, for out of the watery depths close to the bridge slowly emerged a skeletal figure clad in a dripping wet grey garment. Long thin straggly wet hair draped down a gaunt frame which mercifully concealed the face. The being slowly climbed over the bank and headed towards the cottage. Shaking himself out of his stupor, Cavell looked at his watch: 12.50am. What if Stone's clock was fast? Cavell broke out in a cold sweat as he turned around and ran back to the cottage to warn him of the evil approaching. But as he neared the cottage, the entity reached the door and suddenly turned, sensing a being close by. Cavell froze on the spot. The last image before he fainted was a hideous being devoid of flesh, a grinning skull with sunken eyes of vivid orange!

*

Luther Stone had only just retired to bed when he was woken by the sound of persistent knocking on his front door. Glancing at his clock, he saw that it read 1.05pm. Past the witching hour. Probably the traveller seeking further help he thought to himself. As he slid the bolts back and opened the door, his terror-induced scream reverberated around the cottage. For standing in the doorway was the shrunken hideous entity that passed for Rose Manning! As the creature advanced into the cottage, Stone froze on the spot and felt powerless as his assailant closed her long bony fingers around her victim's neck, squeezing the life out of him…

*

It seemed hours had passed before Cavell recovered. As he rose sluggishly to his feet, night was giving way to day. Trying to recall the previous events, he observed that the door to the cottage was wide open. Stone! On entering the cottage, his worst fears were confirmed for spreadeagled on the floor was the late Luther Stone, his eyes bulging like oversized organ stops and protruding unnaturally from the deathly grey pallor of his frightened face. Whether it was the ghastly vision that confronted him after his ill-judged opening of his door, or the deep bruising of the neck, his last moments were no doubt far from pleasant. Looking up at the clock he saw that the time was five minutes later than that on Cavell's watch which he knew was correct. Stone had opened the door to his ghostly assassin believing the witching hour had passed but had in fact conducted the deed too soon, and had paid the ultimate price. Rose Manning had gained her revenge. Perhaps Stone had been economical with the truth surrounding the death of his best friend thought Cavell as he made his way successfully back to civilisation courtesy of the directions of the late Luther Stone.

ABOUT THE AUTHOR

John Dyble was born in Great Yarmouth 1951 and, following a productive period of education, enjoyed a successful career in the Civil Service before retiring in 2011. Since then he has kept himself actively engaged in a variety of pursuits, including five-a-side football twice a week which he continues to enjoy and daily power walking. Other leisure time is spent travelling, landscape gardening, listening to rock music and reading, especially tales of the supernatural. He is particularly fond of military history, loves driving and is also a supporter of Norwich City football club.

Printed in Great Britain
by Amazon

26251109R00076